THE HEART
A GRAPHIC NOVEL TOUR

written by
Joeming Dunn
illustrated by
Rod Espinosa

visit us at
www.abdopublishing.com

Published by Magic Wagon, a division of the ABDO Group, 8000 West 78th Street, Edina, Minnesota 55439. Copyright © 2010 by Abdo Consulting Group, Inc. International copyrights reserved in all countries. All rights reserved. No part of this book may be reproduced in any form without written permission from the publisher.

Graphic Planet™ is a trademark and logo of Magic Wagon.

Printed in the United States.

 Manufactured with paper containing at least 10% post-consumer waste

Text by Joeming Dunn
Illustrated by Rod Espinosa
Colored and lettered by Rod Espinosa
Edited by Stephanie Hedlund
Interior layout and design by Antarctic Press
Cover art by Rod Espinosa
Cover design by Neil Klinepier

Library of Congress Cataloging-in-Publication Data

Dunn, Joeming W.
  The heart : a graphic novel tour / by Joeming Dunn ; illustrated by Rod Espinosa.
     p. cm. -- (Graphic adventures. The human body)
  Includes bibliographical references and index.
  ISBN 978-1-60270-685-9 (alk. paper)
 1. Heart--Juvenile literature. 2. Graphic novels--Juvenile literature. I. Espinosa, Rod, ill. II. Title.
  QP111.6.D86 2010
  612.1'7--dc22
                        2009017851

TABLE of CONTENTS

Meet the Explorers..4

Have a Heart!...5

The Heart: A Diagram..28

Fun Facts..29

Glossary 30

Web Sites 30

About the Author...31

About the Illustrator...31

Index 32

Meet the Explorers

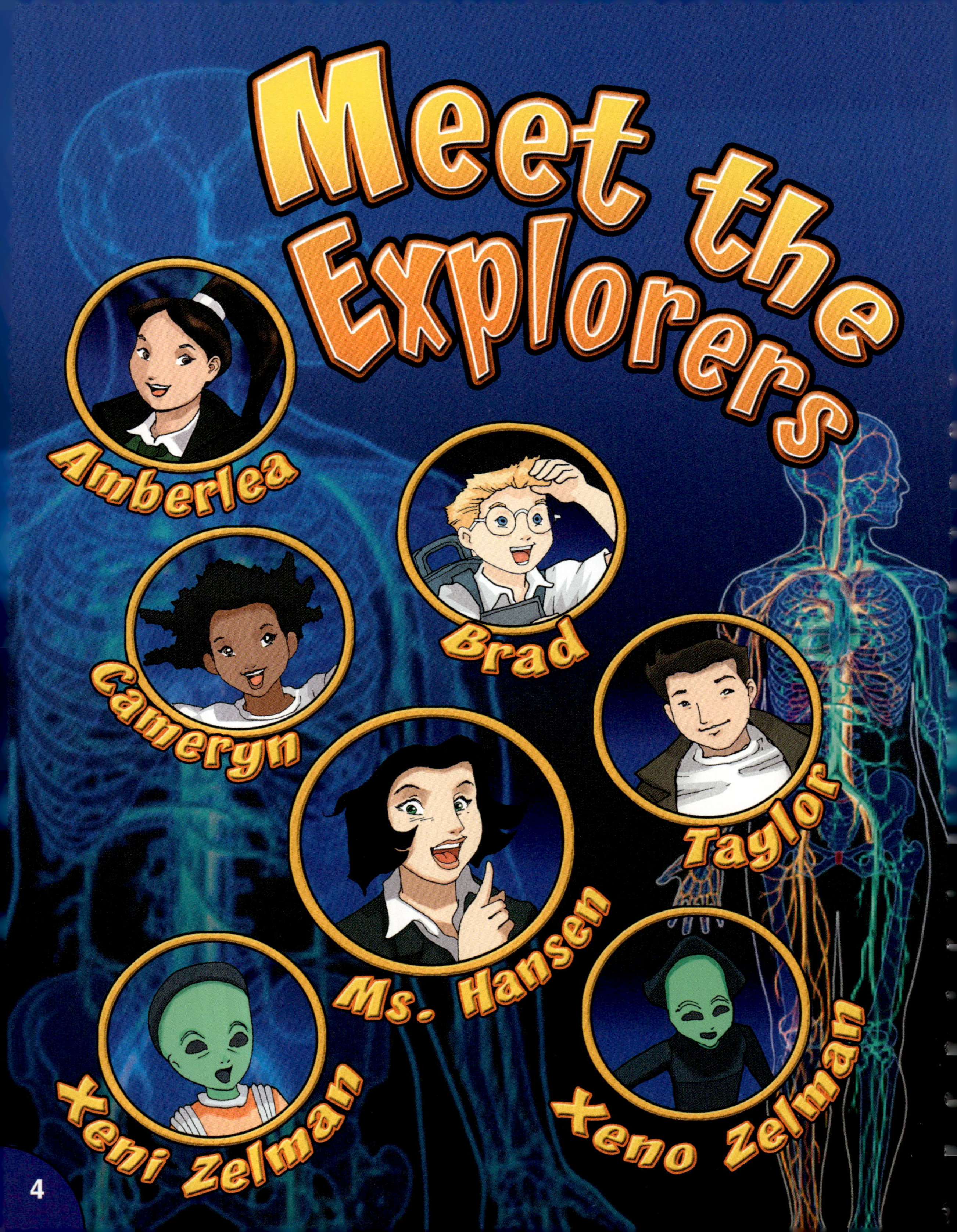
Amberlea
Brad
Cameryn
Taylor
Ms. Hansen
Xeni Zelman
Xeno Zelman

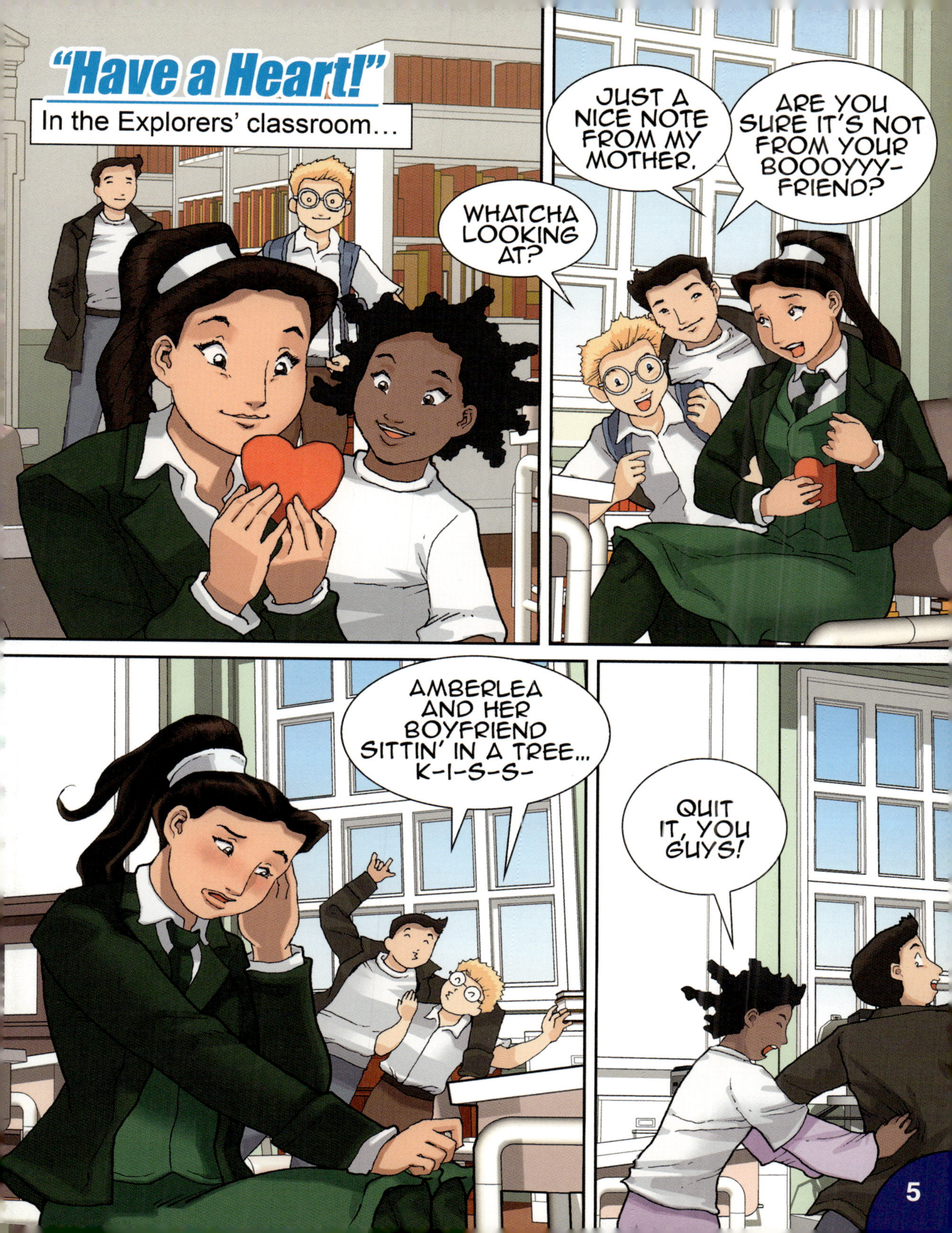
"Have a Heart!"
In the Explorers' classroom...
WHATCHA LOOKING AT?
JUST A NICE NOTE FROM MY MOTHER.
ARE YOU SURE IT'S NOT FROM YOUR BOOOYYY-FRIEND?
AMBERLEA AND HER BOYFRIEND SITTIN' IN A TREE... K-I-S-S-
QUIT IT, YOU GUYS!

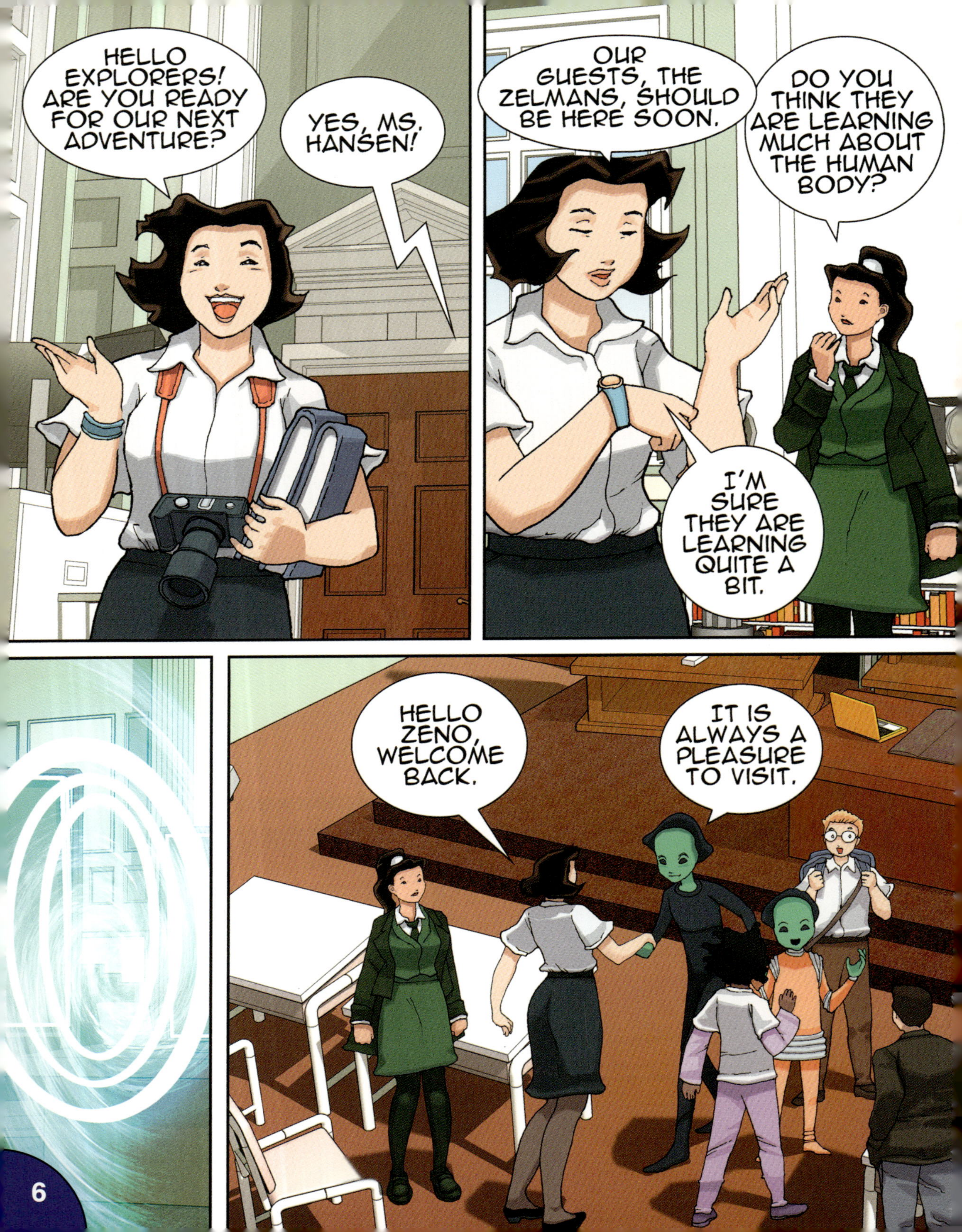
HELLO EXPLORERS! ARE YOU READY FOR OUR NEXT ADVENTURE?
YES, MS. HANSEN!
OUR GUESTS, THE ZELMANS, SHOULD BE HERE SOON.
DO YOU THINK THEY ARE LEARNING MUCH ABOUT THE HUMAN BODY?
I'M SURE THEY ARE LEARNING QUITE A BIT.
HELLO ZENO, WELCOME BACK.
IT IS ALWAYS A PLEASURE TO VISIT.

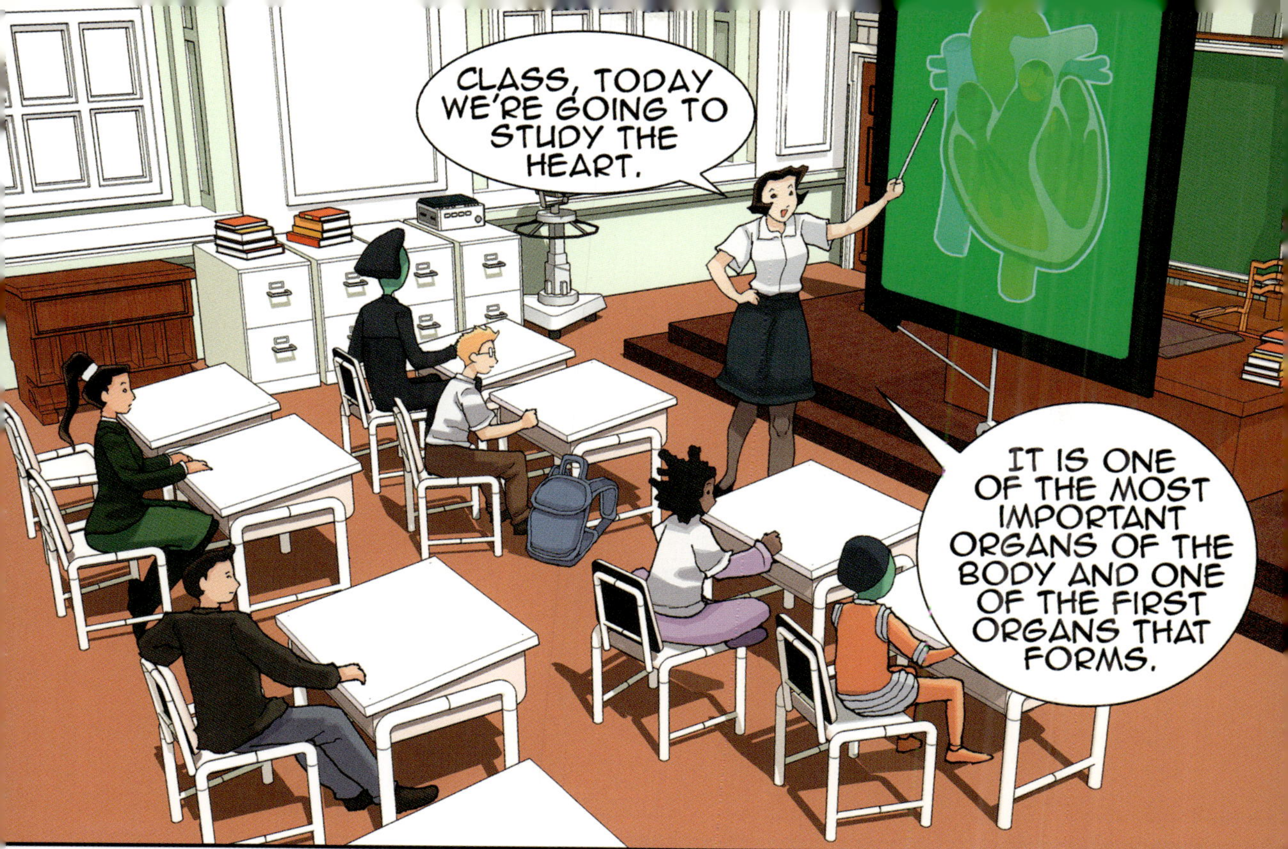
CLASS, TODAY WE'RE GOING TO STUDY THE HEART.
IT IS ONE OF THE MOST IMPORTANT ORGANS OF THE BODY AND ONE OF THE FIRST ORGANS THAT FORMS.

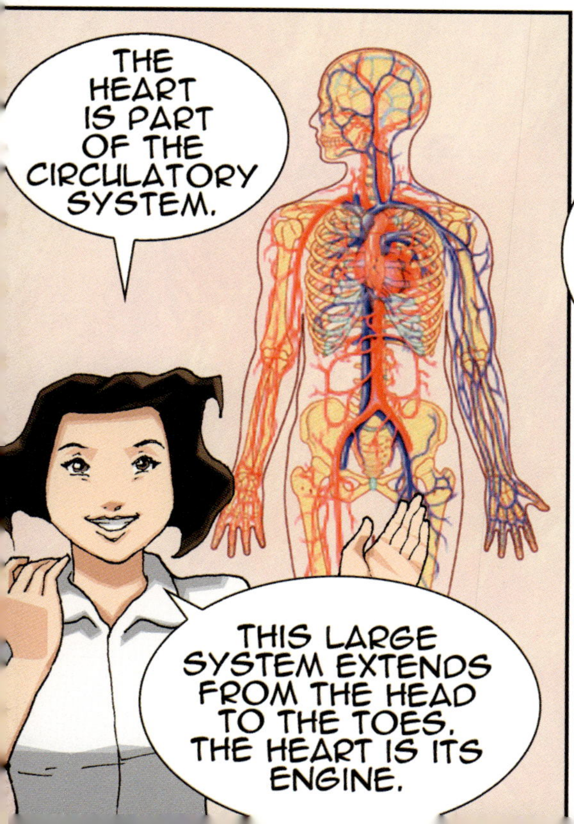
THE HEART IS PART OF THE CIRCULATORY SYSTEM.
THIS LARGE SYSTEM EXTENDS FROM THE HEAD TO THE TOES. THE HEART IS ITS ENGINE.

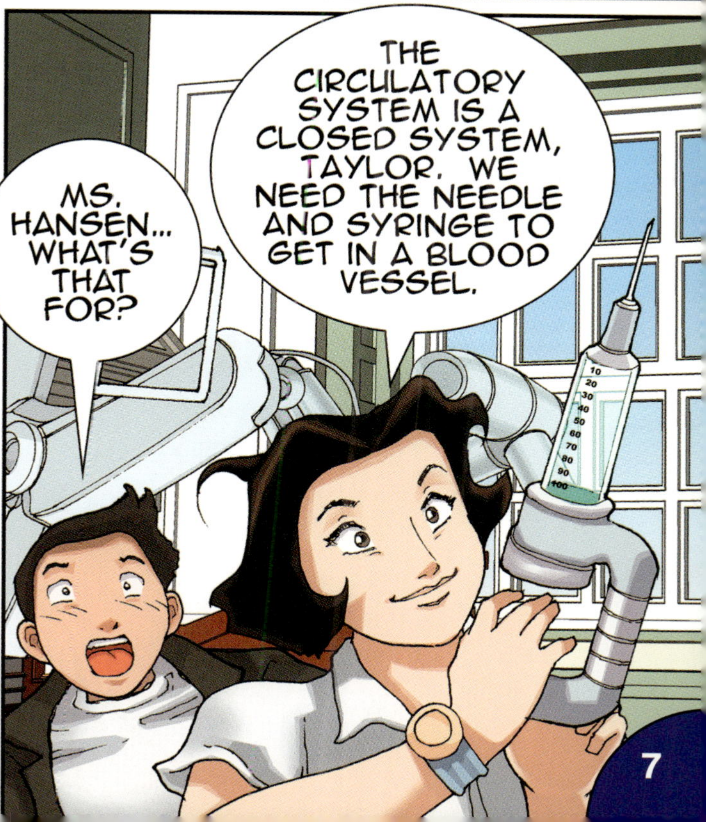
MS. HANSEN... WHAT'S THAT FOR?
THE CIRCULATORY SYSTEM IS A CLOSED SYSTEM, TAYLOR. WE NEED THE NEEDLE AND SYRINGE TO GET IN A BLOOD VESSEL.

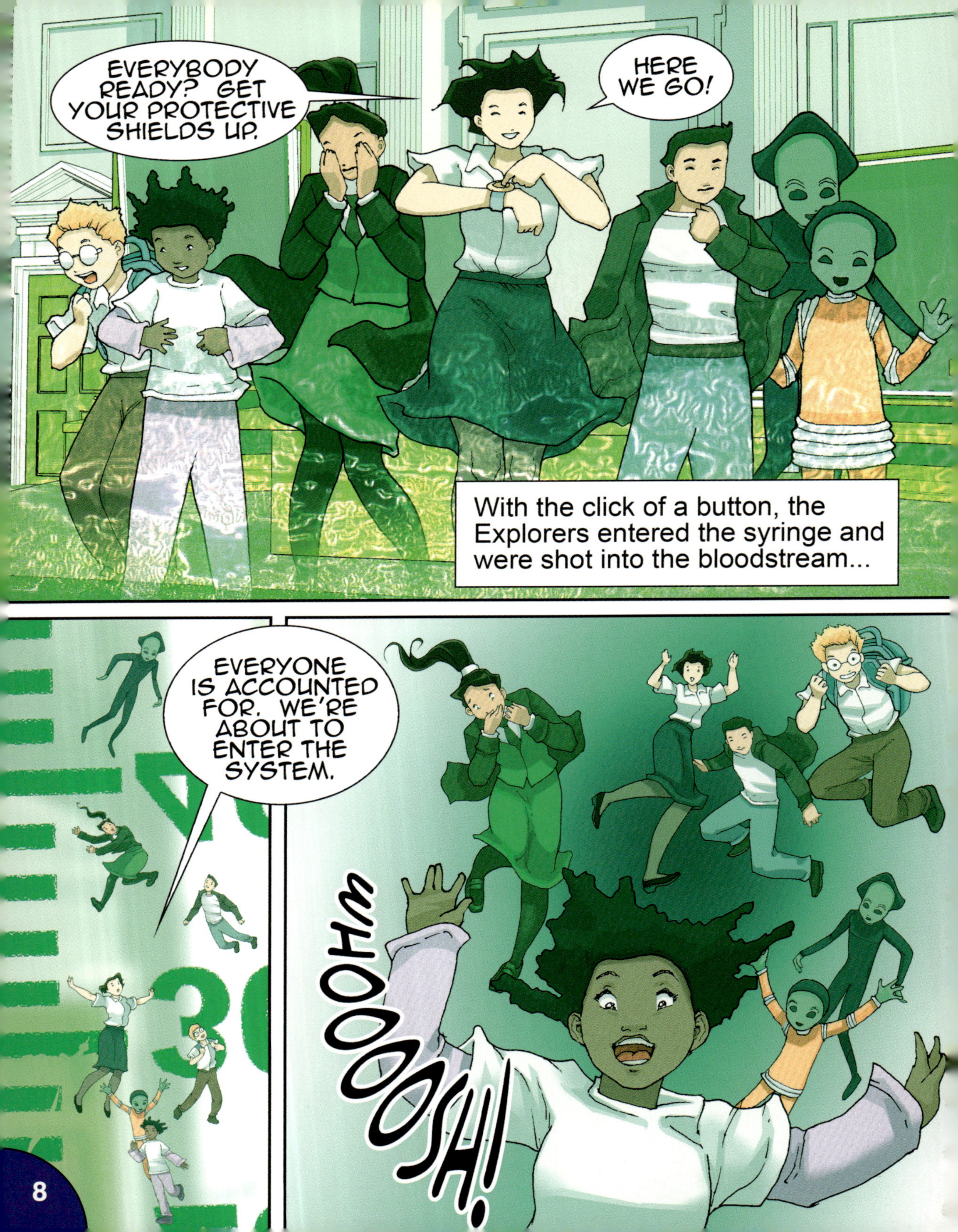
EVERYBODY READY? GET YOUR PROTECTIVE SHIELDS UP.
HERE WE GO!
With the click of a button, the Explorers entered the syringe and were shot into the bloodstream...
EVERYONE IS ACCOUNTED FOR. WE'RE ABOUT TO ENTER THE SYSTEM.
WHOOOOSH!

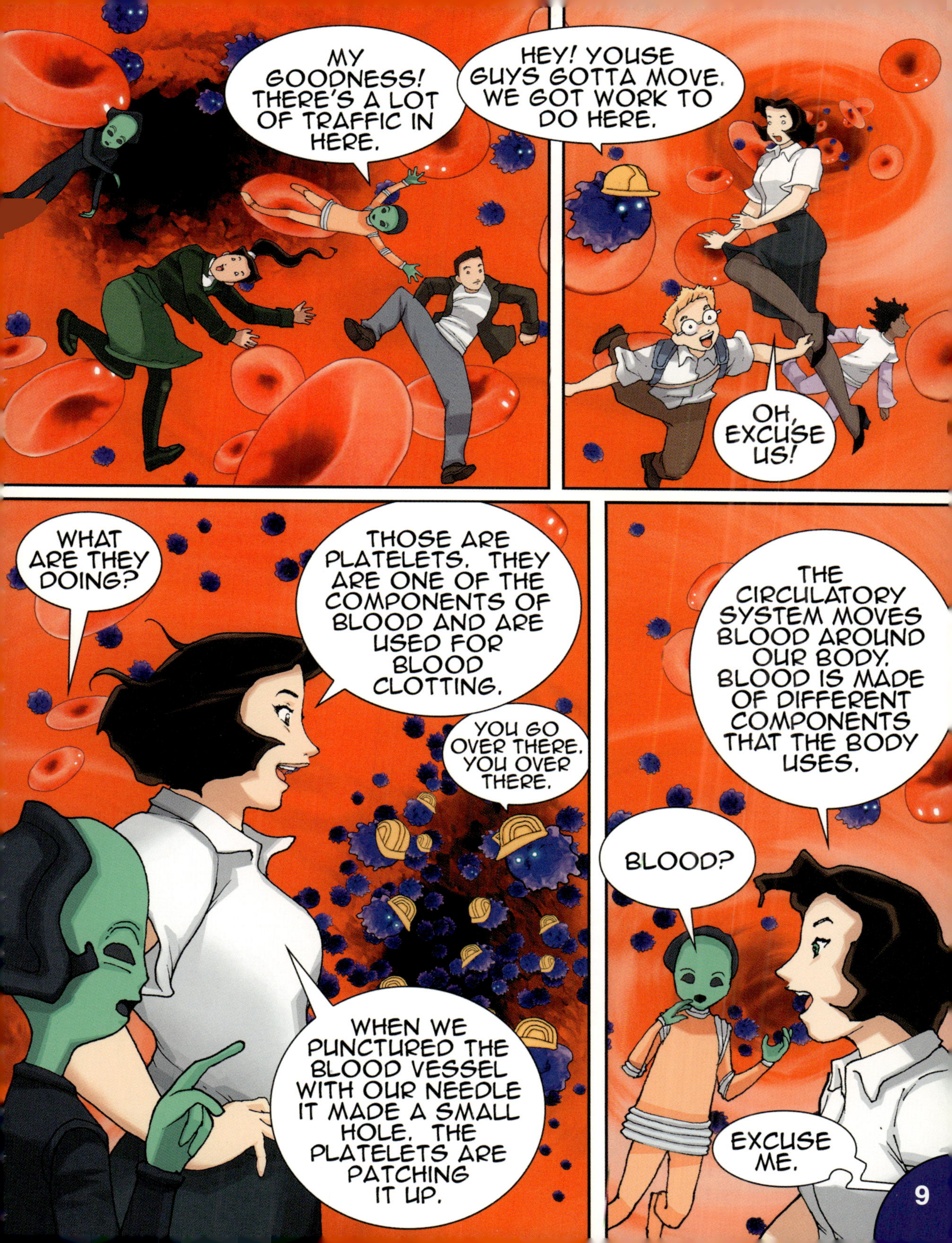
MY GOODNESS! THERE'S A LOT OF TRAFFIC IN HERE.
HEY! YOUSE GUYS GOTTA MOVE. WE GOT WORK TO DO HERE.
OH, EXCUSE US!
WHAT ARE THEY DOING?
THOSE ARE PLATELETS. THEY ARE ONE OF THE COMPONENTS OF BLOOD AND ARE USED FOR BLOOD CLOTTING.
YOU GO OVER THERE. YOU OVER THERE.
WHEN WE PUNCTURED THE BLOOD VESSEL WITH OUR NEEDLE IT MADE A SMALL HOLE. THE PLATELETS ARE PATCHING IT UP.
THE CIRCULATORY SYSTEM MOVES BLOOD AROUND OUR BODY. BLOOD IS MADE OF DIFFERENT COMPONENTS THAT THE BODY USES.
BLOOD?
EXCUSE ME.

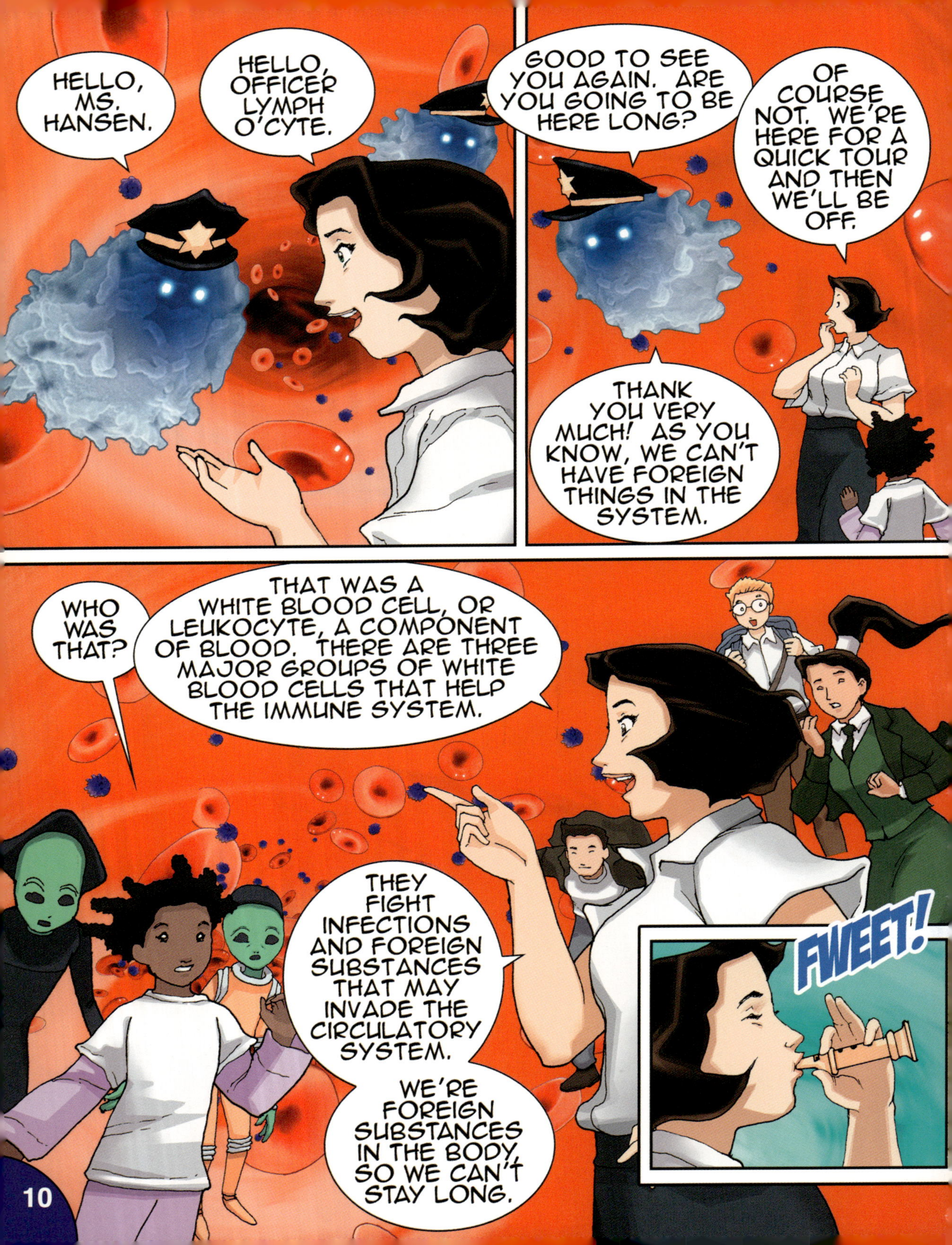
HELLO, MS. HANSEN.
HELLO, OFFICER LYMPH O'CYTE.
GOOD TO SEE YOU AGAIN. ARE YOU GOING TO BE HERE LONG?
OF COURSE NOT. WE'RE HERE FOR A QUICK TOUR AND THEN WE'LL BE OFF.
THANK YOU VERY MUCH! AS YOU KNOW, WE CAN'T HAVE FOREIGN THINGS IN THE SYSTEM.
WHO WAS THAT?
THAT WAS A WHITE BLOOD CELL, OR LEUKOCYTE, A COMPONENT OF BLOOD. THERE ARE THREE MAJOR GROUPS OF WHITE BLOOD CELLS THAT HELP THE IMMUNE SYSTEM.
THEY FIGHT INFECTIONS AND FOREIGN SUBSTANCES THAT MAY INVADE THE CIRCULATORY SYSTEM.
WE'RE FOREIGN SUBSTANCES IN THE BODY, SO WE CAN'T STAY LONG.
FWEET!

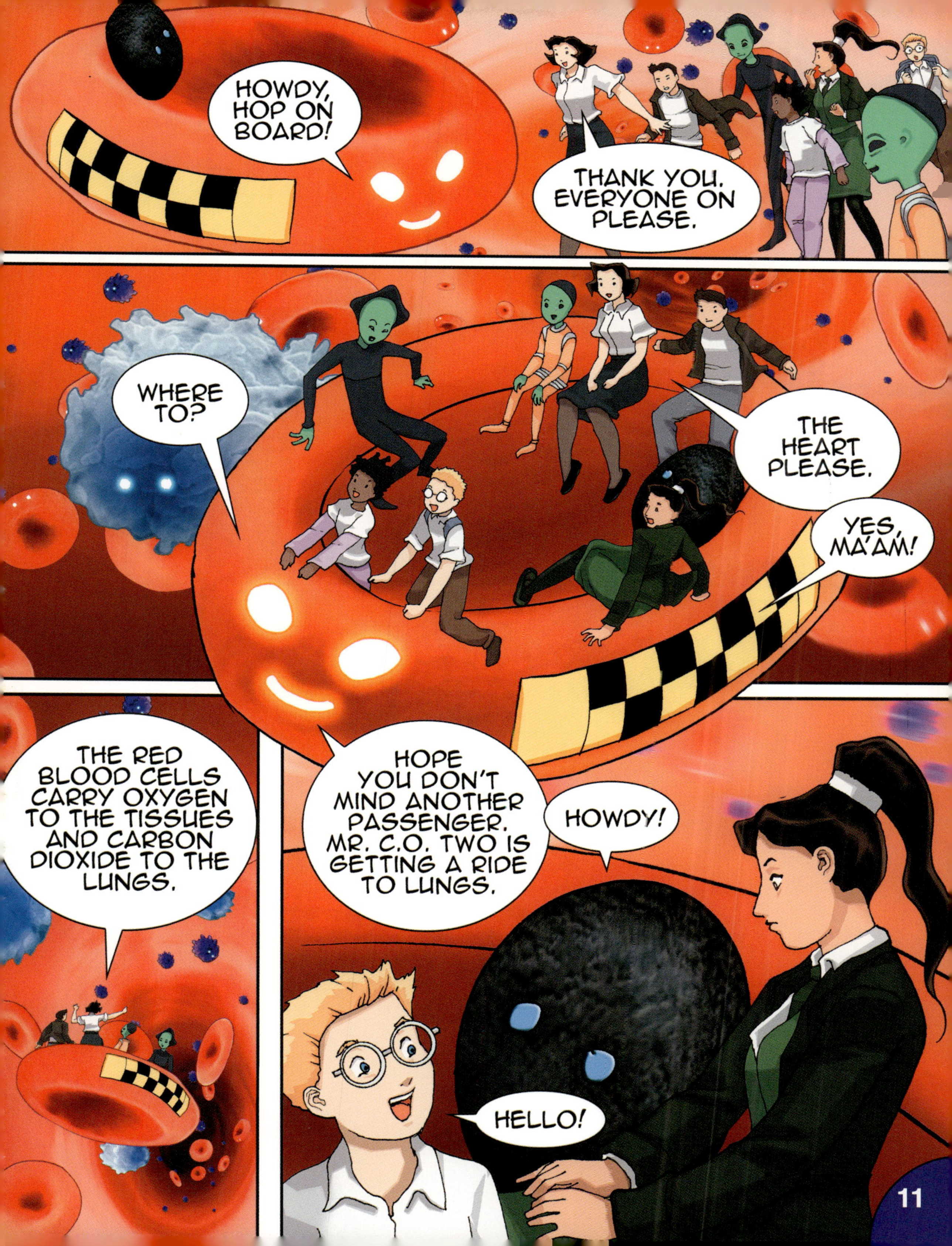
HOWDY, HOP ON BOARD!
THANK YOU. EVERYONE ON PLEASE.
WHERE TO?
THE HEART PLEASE.
YES, MA'AM!
THE RED BLOOD CELLS CARRY OXYGEN TO THE TISSUES AND CARBON DIOXIDE TO THE LUNGS.
HOPE YOU DON'T MIND ANOTHER PASSENGER. MR. C.O. TWO IS GETTING A RIDE TO LUNGS.
HOWDY!
HELLO!

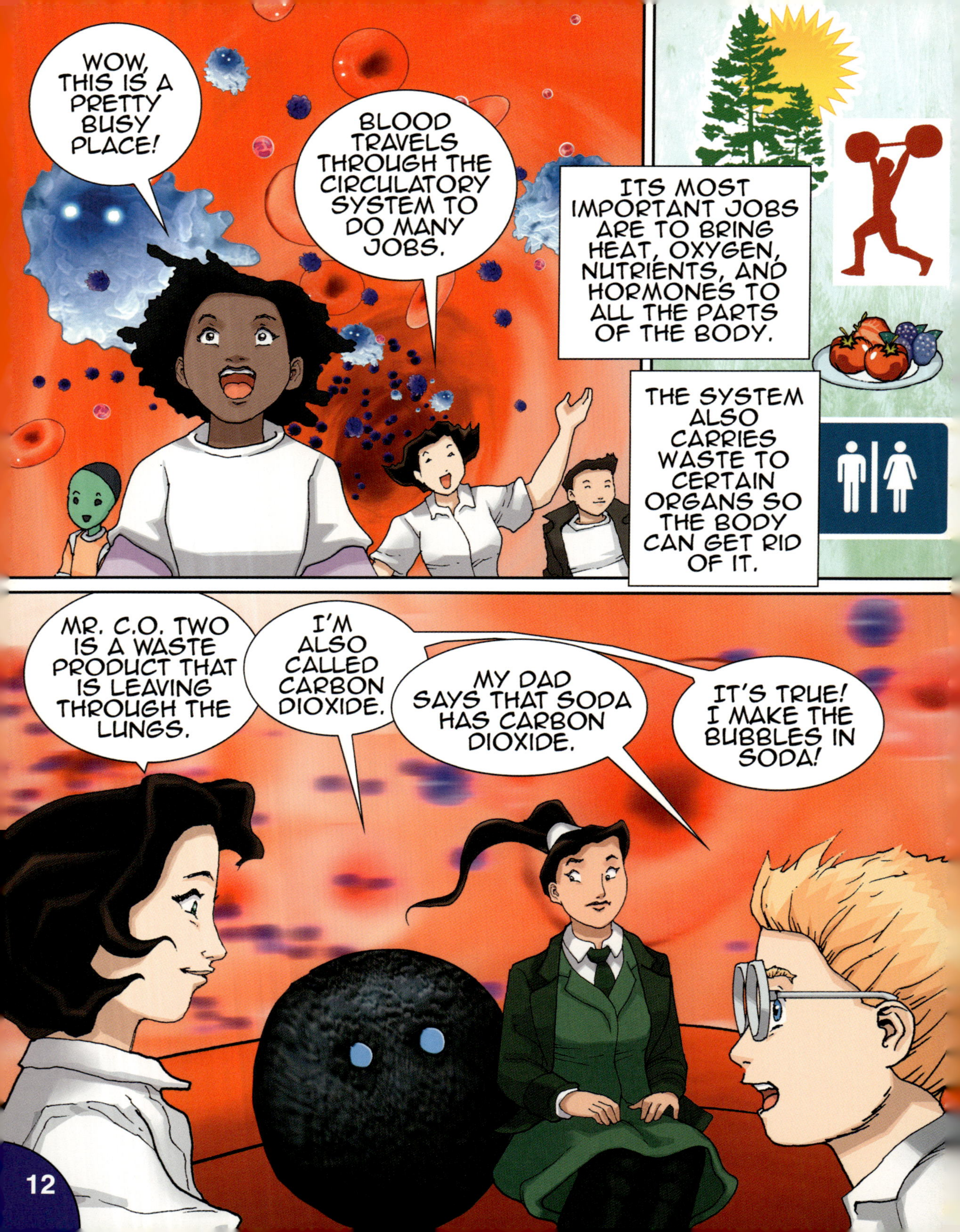
WOW, THIS IS A PRETTY BUSY PLACE!
BLOOD TRAVELS THROUGH THE CIRCULATORY SYSTEM TO DO MANY JOBS.
ITS MOST IMPORTANT JOBS ARE TO BRING HEAT, OXYGEN, NUTRIENTS, AND HORMONES TO ALL THE PARTS OF THE BODY.
THE SYSTEM ALSO CARRIES WASTE TO CERTAIN ORGANS SO THE BODY CAN GET RID OF IT.
MR. C.O. TWO IS A WASTE PRODUCT THAT IS LEAVING THROUGH THE LUNGS.
I'M ALSO CALLED CARBON DIOXIDE.
MY DAD SAYS THAT SODA HAS CARBON DIOXIDE.
IT'S TRUE! I MAKE THE BUBBLES IN SODA!

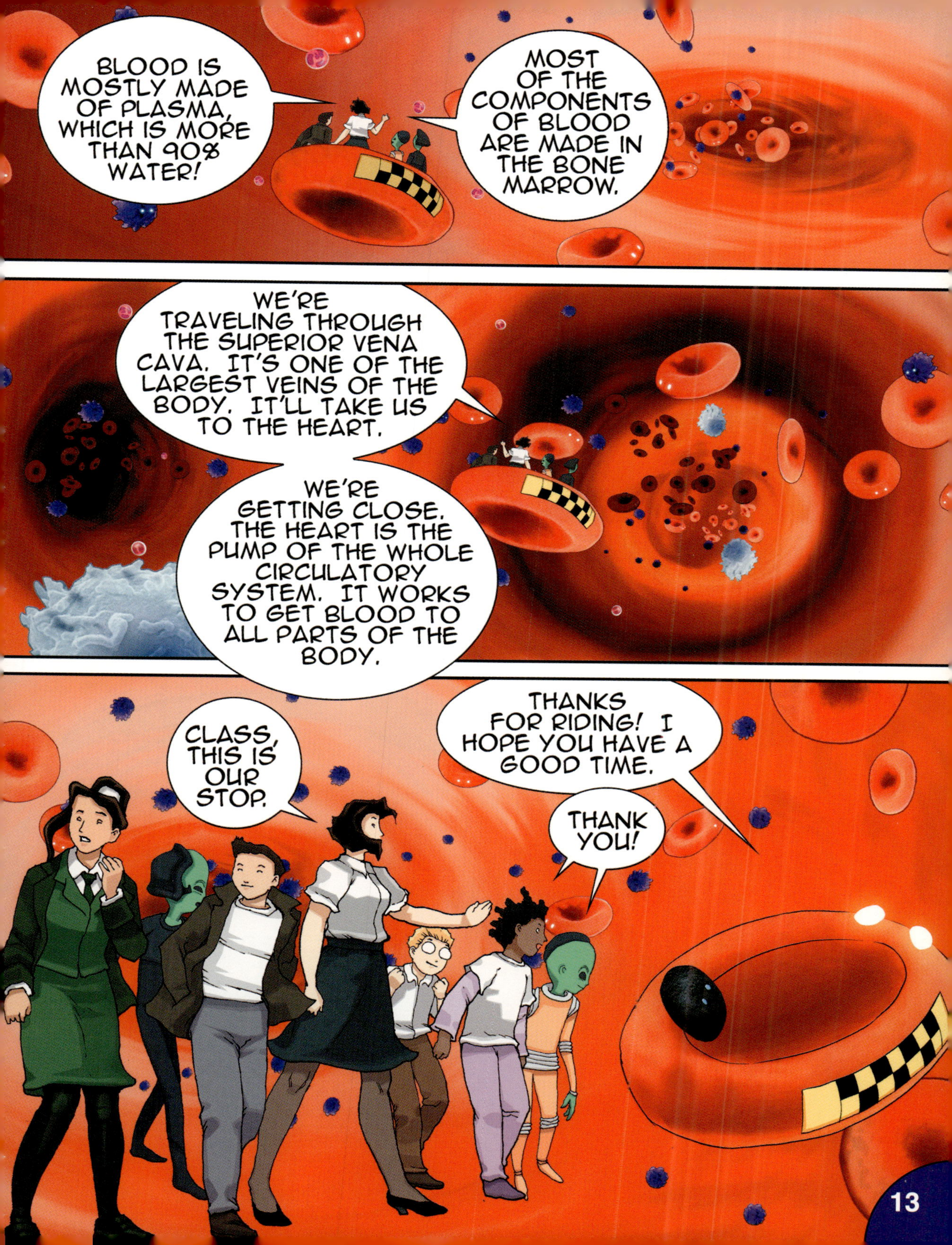
BLOOD IS MOSTLY MADE OF PLASMA, WHICH IS MORE THAN 90% WATER!
MOST OF THE COMPONENTS OF BLOOD ARE MADE IN THE BONE MARROW.
WE'RE TRAVELING THROUGH THE SUPERIOR VENA CAVA. IT'S ONE OF THE LARGEST VEINS OF THE BODY. IT'LL TAKE US TO THE HEART.
WE'RE GETTING CLOSE. THE HEART IS THE PUMP OF THE WHOLE CIRCULATORY SYSTEM. IT WORKS TO GET BLOOD TO ALL PARTS OF THE BODY.
CLASS, THIS IS OUR STOP.
THANKS FOR RIDING! I HOPE YOU HAVE A GOOD TIME.
THANK YOU!

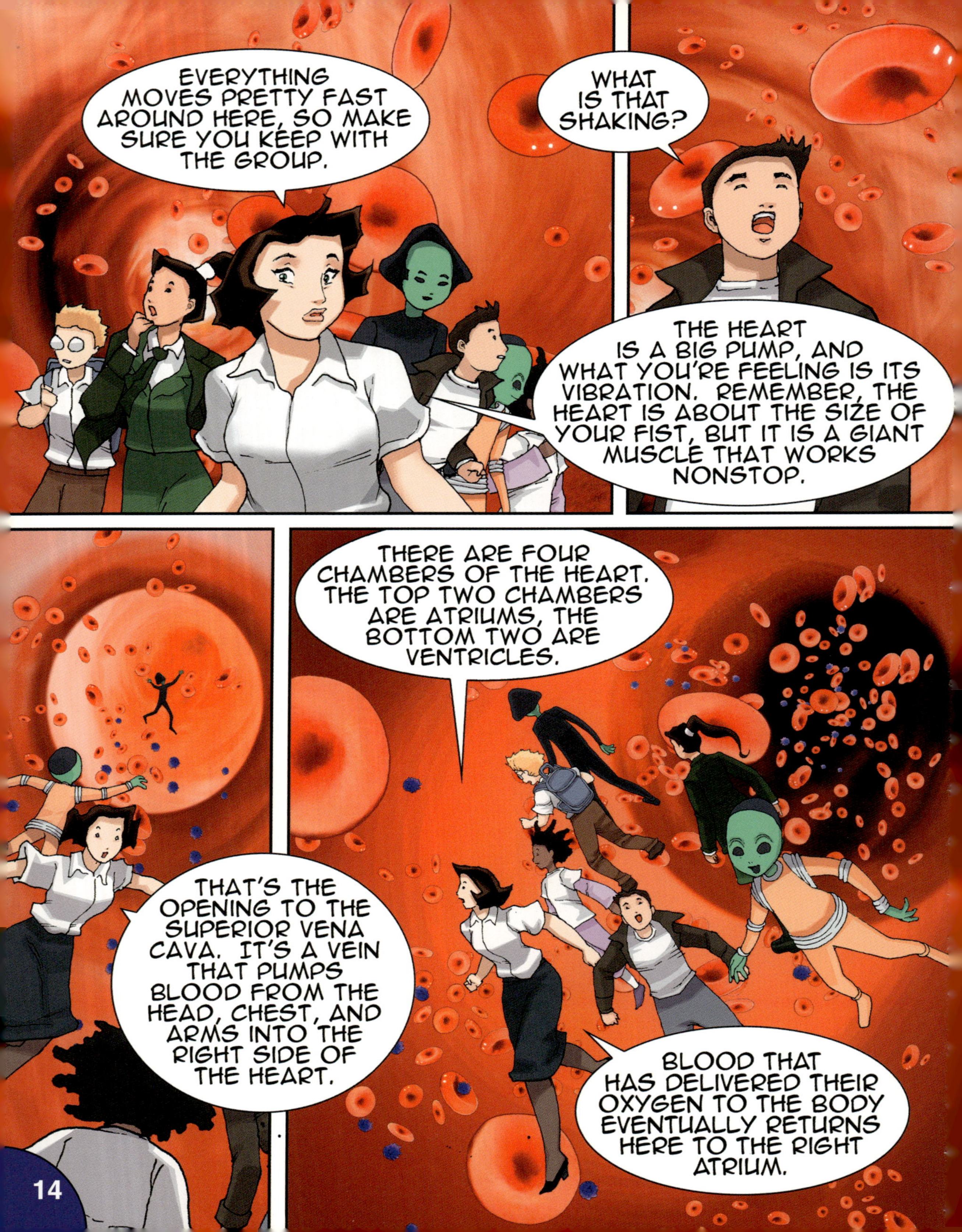
EVERYTHING MOVES PRETTY FAST AROUND HERE, SO MAKE SURE YOU KEEP WITH THE GROUP.
WHAT IS THAT SHAKING?
THE HEART IS A BIG PUMP, AND WHAT YOU'RE FEELING IS ITS VIBRATION. REMEMBER, THE HEART IS ABOUT THE SIZE OF YOUR FIST, BUT IT IS A GIANT MUSCLE THAT WORKS NONSTOP.
THAT'S THE OPENING TO THE SUPERIOR VENA CAVA. IT'S A VEIN THAT PUMPS BLOOD FROM THE HEAD, CHEST, AND ARMS INTO THE RIGHT SIDE OF THE HEART.
THERE ARE FOUR CHAMBERS OF THE HEART. THE TOP TWO CHAMBERS ARE ATRIUMS, THE BOTTOM TWO ARE VENTRICLES.
BLOOD THAT HAS DELIVERED THEIR OXYGEN TO THE BODY EVENTUALLY RETURNS HERE TO THE RIGHT ATRIUM.

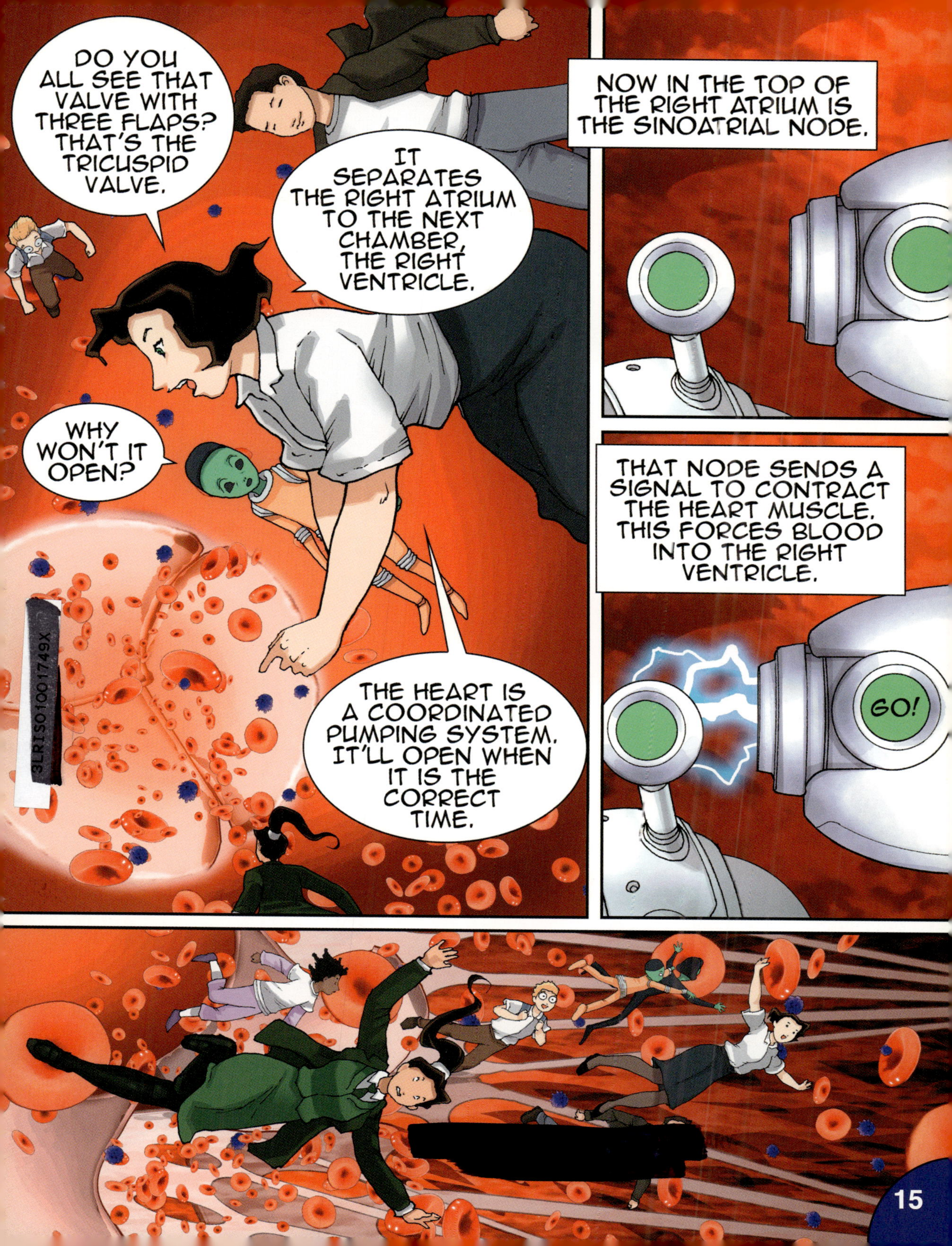
DO YOU ALL SEE THAT VALVE WITH THREE FLAPS? THAT'S THE TRICUSPID VALVE.
IT SEPARATES THE RIGHT ATRIUM TO THE NEXT CHAMBER, THE RIGHT VENTRICLE.
WHY WON'T IT OPEN?
THE HEART IS A COORDINATED PUMPING SYSTEM. IT'LL OPEN WHEN IT IS THE CORRECT TIME.
NOW IN THE TOP OF THE RIGHT ATRIUM IS THE SINOATRIAL NODE.
THAT NODE SENDS A SIGNAL TO CONTRACT THE HEART MUSCLE. THIS FORCES BLOOD INTO THE RIGHT VENTRICLE.
GO!

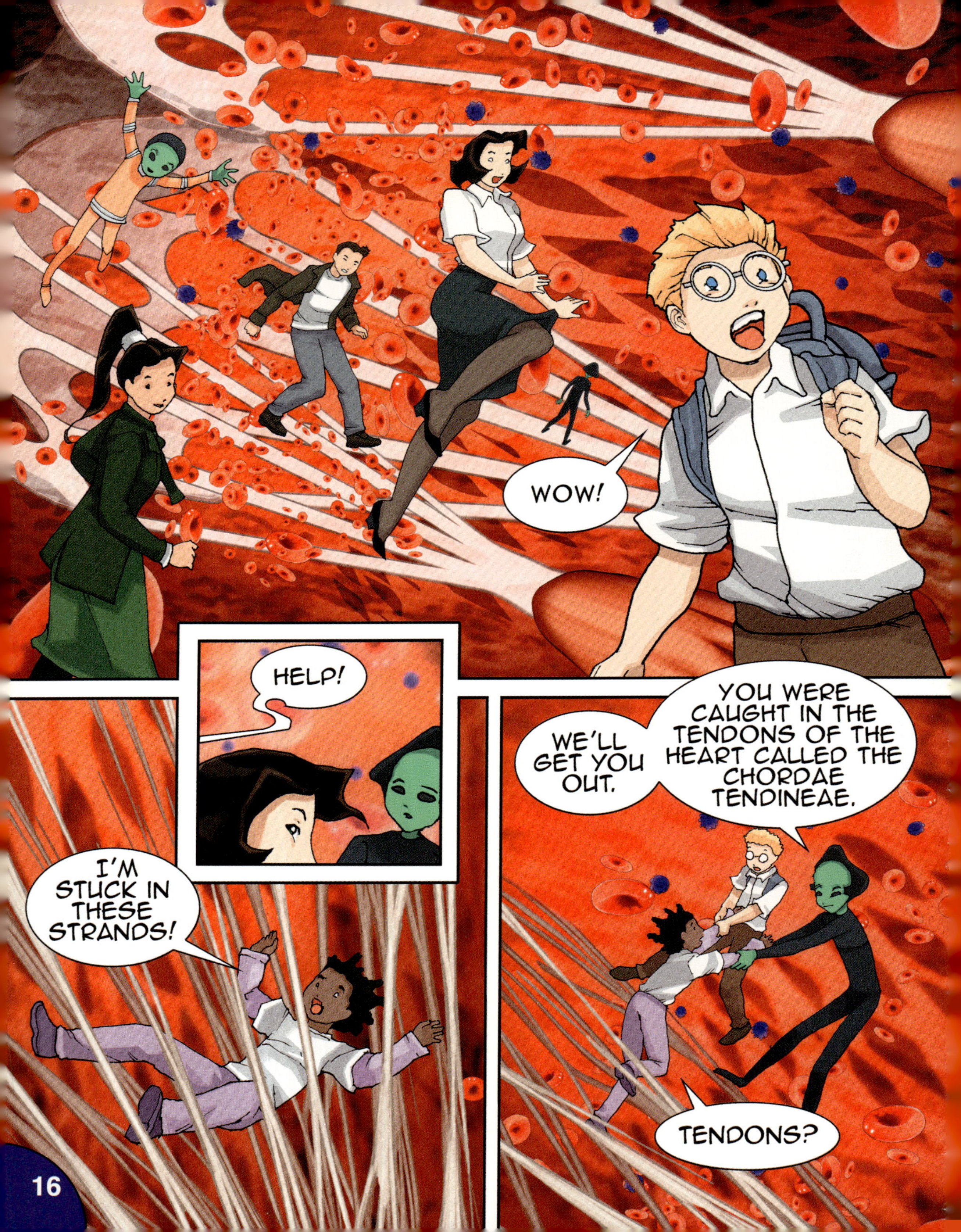
WOW!
HELP!
I'M STUCK IN THESE STRANDS!
WE'LL GET YOU OUT.
YOU WERE CAUGHT IN THE TENDONS OF THE HEART CALLED THE CHORDAE TENDINEAE.
TENDONS?

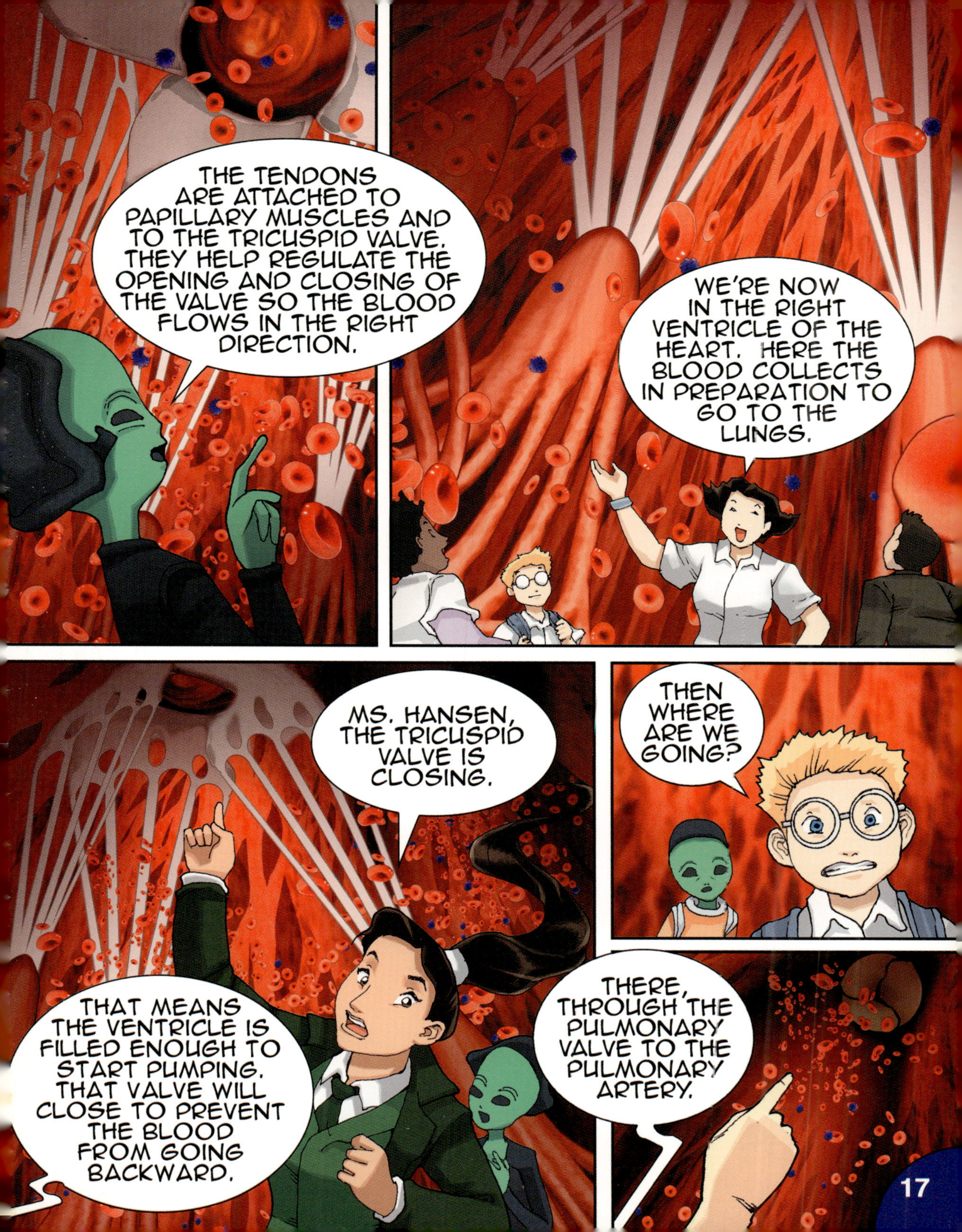
THE TENDONS ARE ATTACHED TO PAPILLARY MUSCLES AND TO THE TRICUSPID VALVE. THEY HELP REGULATE THE OPENING AND CLOSING OF THE VALVE SO THE BLOOD FLOWS IN THE RIGHT DIRECTION.
WE'RE NOW IN THE RIGHT VENTRICLE OF THE HEART. HERE THE BLOOD COLLECTS IN PREPARATION TO GO TO THE LUNGS.
MS. HANSEN, THE TRICUSPID VALVE IS CLOSING.
THAT MEANS THE VENTRICLE IS FILLED ENOUGH TO START PUMPING. THAT VALVE WILL CLOSE TO PREVENT THE BLOOD FROM GOING BACKWARD.
THEN WHERE ARE WE GOING?
THERE, THROUGH THE PULMONARY VALVE TO THE PULMONARY ARTERY.

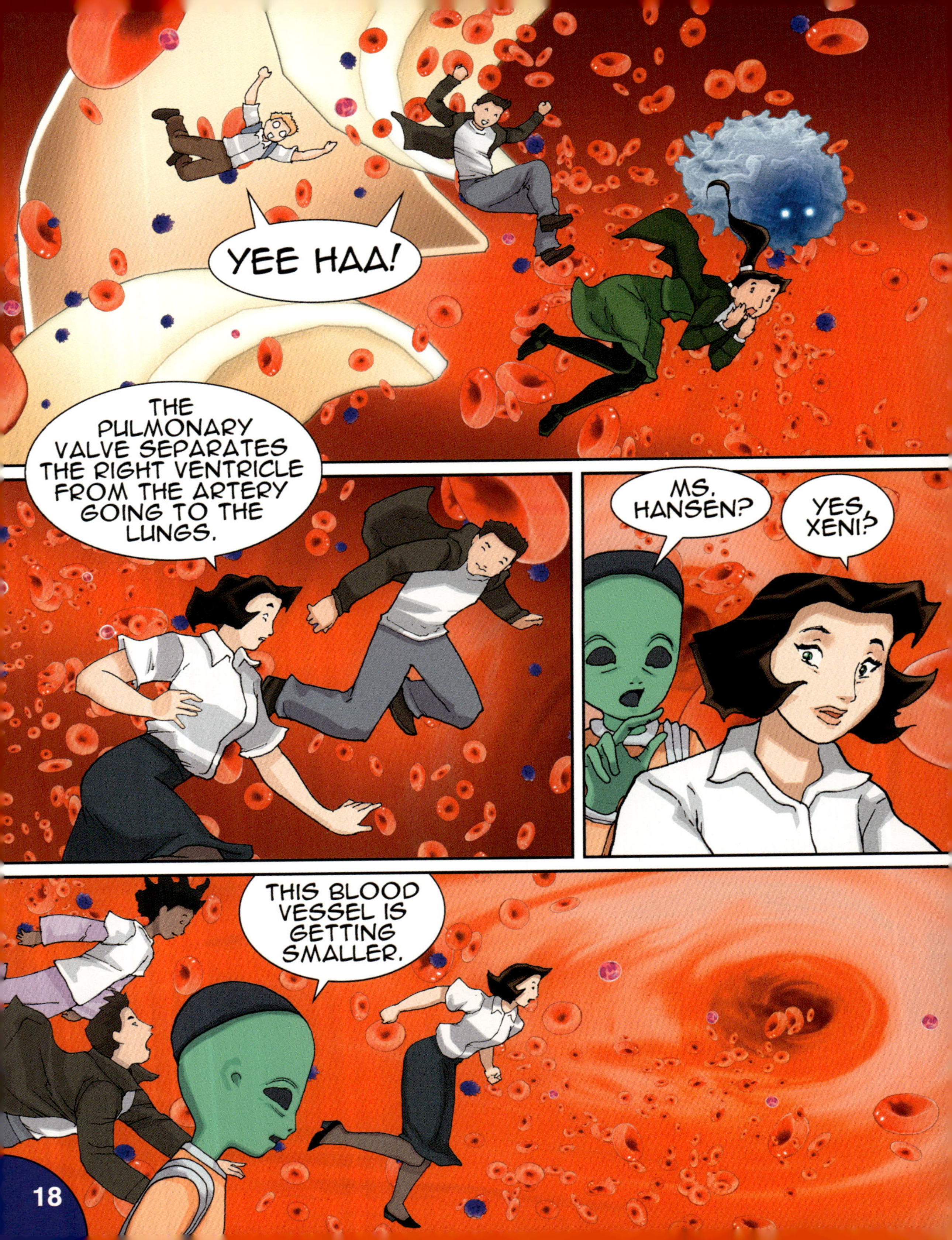
YEE HAA!
THE PULMONARY VALVE SEPARATES THE RIGHT VENTRICLE FROM THE ARTERY GOING TO THE LUNGS.
MS. HANSEN?
YES, XENI?
THIS BLOOD VESSEL IS GETTING SMALLER.

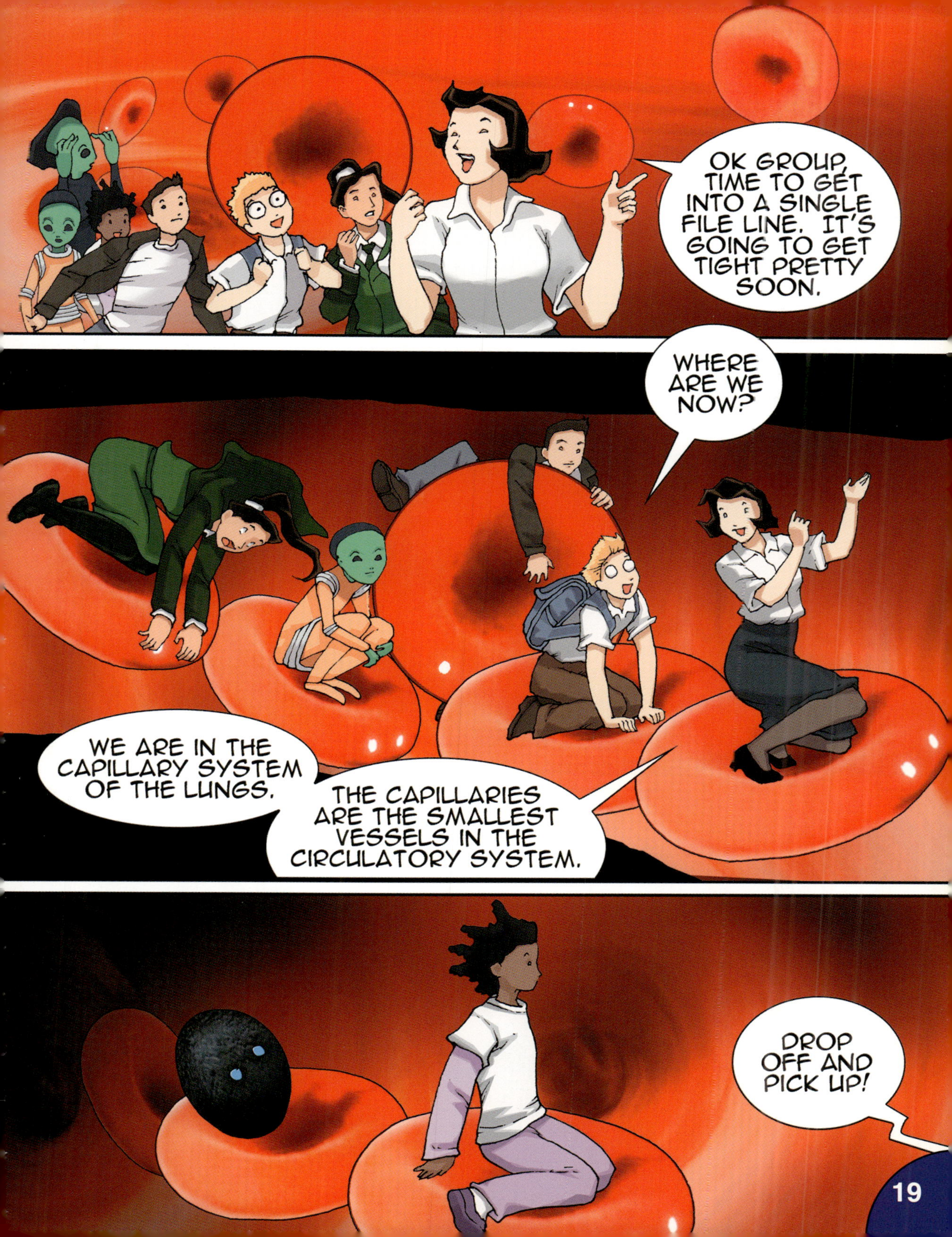
OK GROUP, TIME TO GET INTO A SINGLE FILE LINE. IT'S GOING TO GET TIGHT PRETTY SOON.
WHERE ARE WE NOW?
WE ARE IN THE CAPILLARY SYSTEM OF THE LUNGS.
THE CAPILLARIES ARE THE SMALLEST VESSELS IN THE CIRCULATORY SYSTEM.
DROP OFF AND PICK UP!

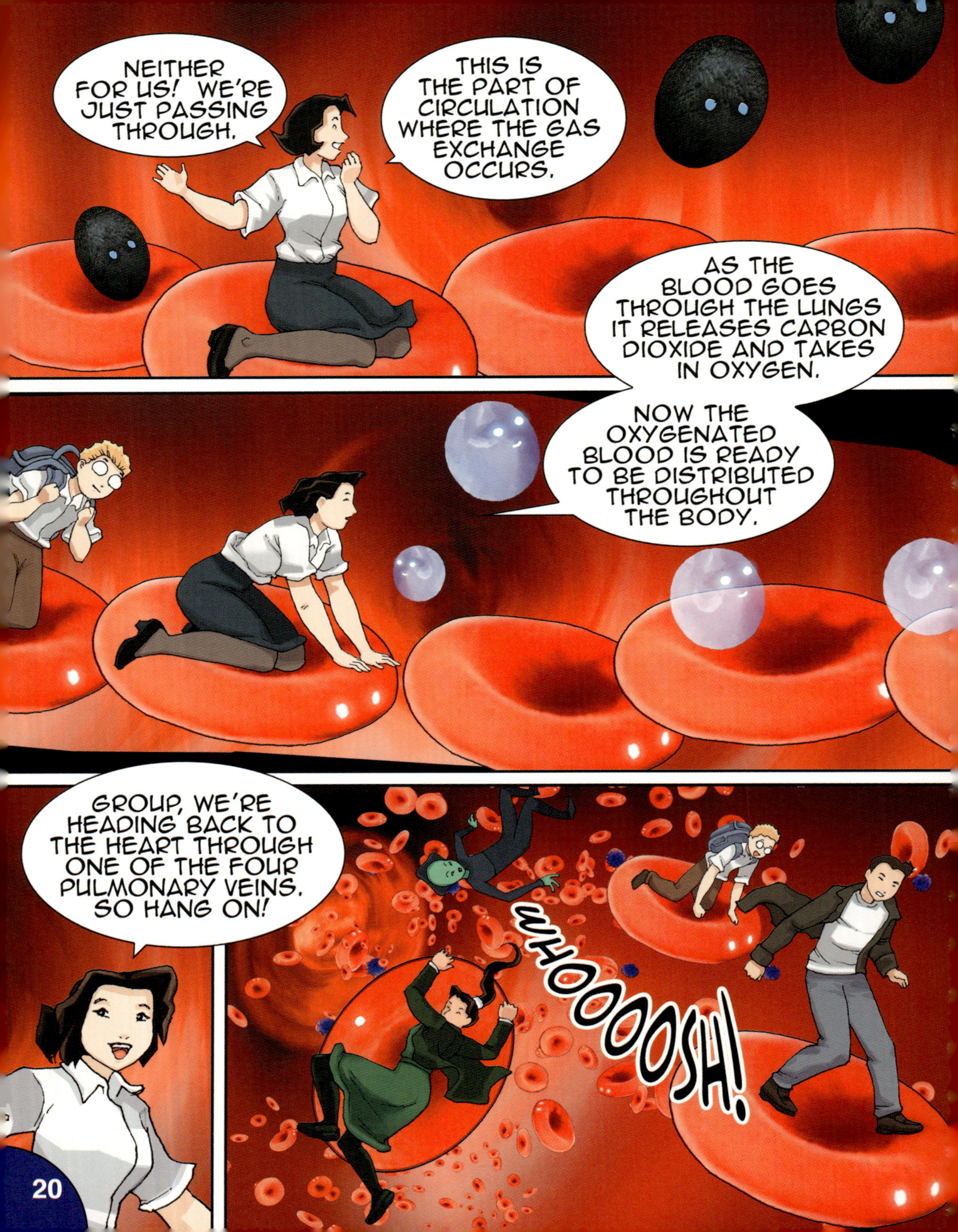
NEITHER FOR US! WE'RE JUST PASSING THROUGH.
THIS IS THE PART OF CIRCULATION WHERE THE GAS EXCHANGE OCCURS.
AS THE BLOOD GOES THROUGH THE LUNGS IT RELEASES CARBON DIOXIDE AND TAKES IN OXYGEN.
NOW THE OXYGENATED BLOOD IS READY TO BE DISTRIBUTED THROUGHOUT THE BODY.
GROUP, WE'RE HEADING BACK TO THE HEART THROUGH ONE OF THE FOUR PULMONARY VEINS. SO HANG ON!
WHOOOOSH!

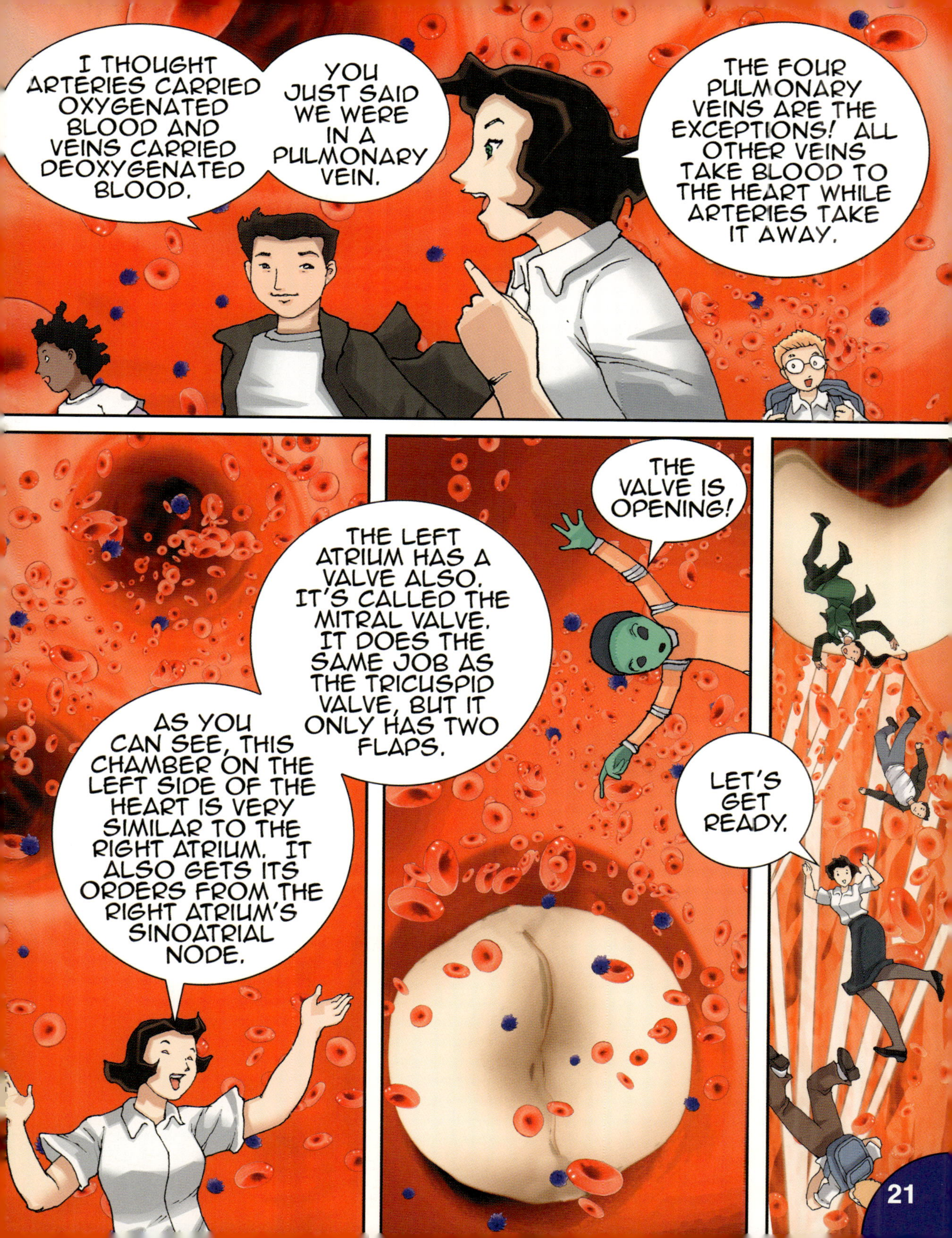

I THOUGHT ARTERIES CARRIED OXYGENATED BLOOD AND VEINS CARRIED DEOXYGENATED BLOOD.
YOU JUST SAID WE WERE IN A PULMONARY VEIN.
THE FOUR PULMONARY VEINS ARE THE EXCEPTIONS! ALL OTHER VEINS TAKE BLOOD TO THE HEART WHILE ARTERIES TAKE IT AWAY.
AS YOU CAN SEE, THIS CHAMBER ON THE LEFT SIDE OF THE HEART IS VERY SIMILAR TO THE RIGHT ATRIUM. IT ALSO GETS ITS ORDERS FROM THE RIGHT ATRIUM'S SINOATRIAL NODE.
THE LEFT ATRIUM HAS A VALVE ALSO. IT'S CALLED THE MITRAL VALVE. IT DOES THE SAME JOB AS THE TRICUSPID VALVE, BUT IT ONLY HAS TWO FLAPS.
THE VALVE IS OPENING!
LET'S GET READY.

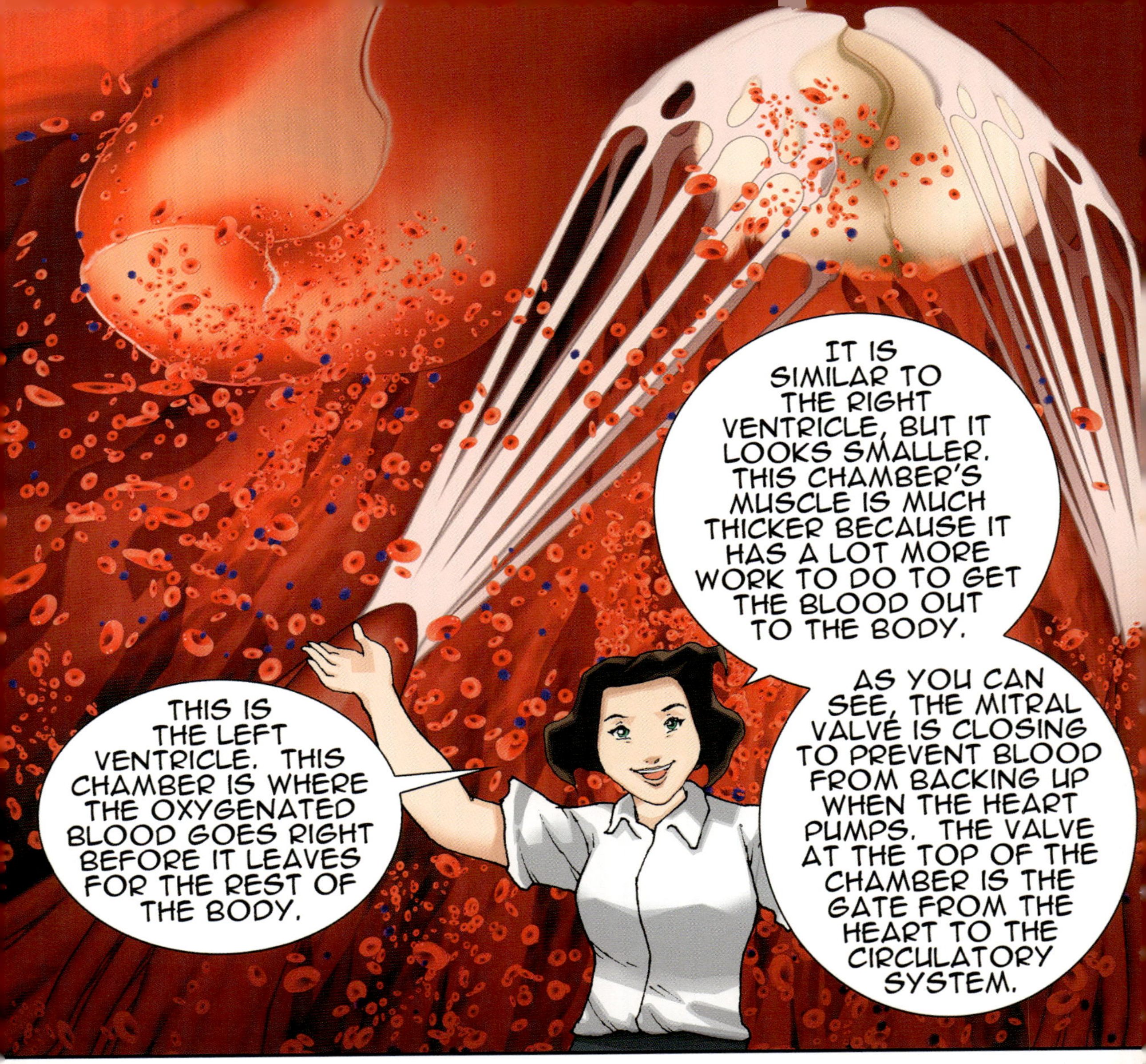
THIS IS THE LEFT VENTRICLE. THIS CHAMBER IS WHERE THE OXYGENATED BLOOD GOES RIGHT BEFORE IT LEAVES FOR THE REST OF THE BODY.
IT IS SIMILAR TO THE RIGHT VENTRICLE, BUT IT LOOKS SMALLER. THIS CHAMBER'S MUSCLE IS MUCH THICKER BECAUSE IT HAS A LOT MORE WORK TO DO TO GET THE BLOOD OUT TO THE BODY.
AS YOU CAN SEE, THE MITRAL VALVE IS CLOSING TO PREVENT BLOOD FROM BACKING UP WHEN THE HEART PUMPS. THE VALVE AT THE TOP OF THE CHAMBER IS THE GATE FROM THE HEART TO THE CIRCULATORY SYSTEM.

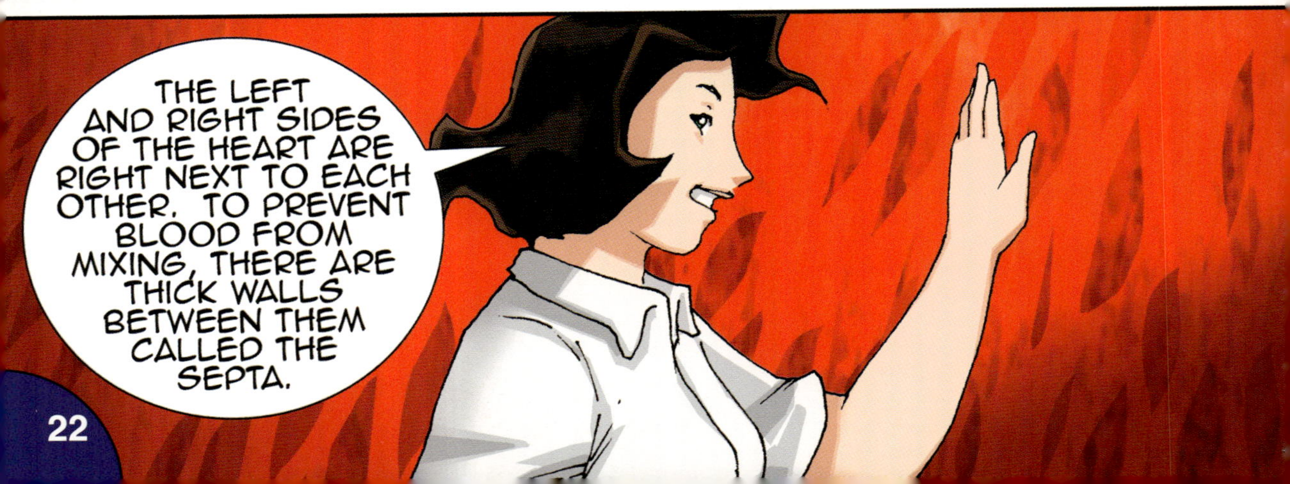
THE LEFT AND RIGHT SIDES OF THE HEART ARE RIGHT NEXT TO EACH OTHER. TO PREVENT BLOOD FROM MIXING, THERE ARE THICK WALLS BETWEEN THEM CALLED THE SEPTA.

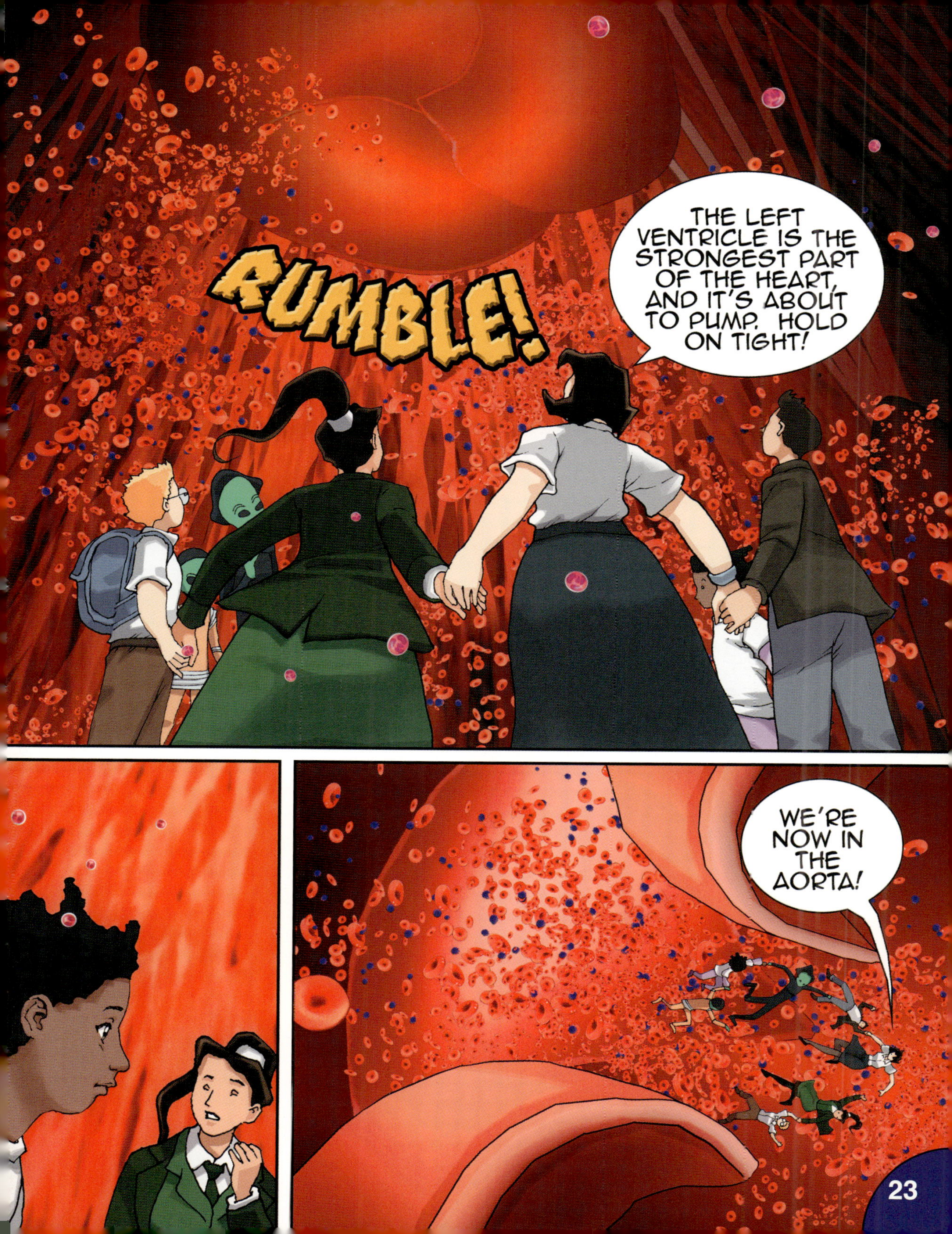
RUMBLE!
THE LEFT VENTRICLE IS THE STRONGEST PART OF THE HEART, AND IT'S ABOUT TO PUMP. HOLD ON TIGHT!
WE'RE NOW IN THE AORTA!

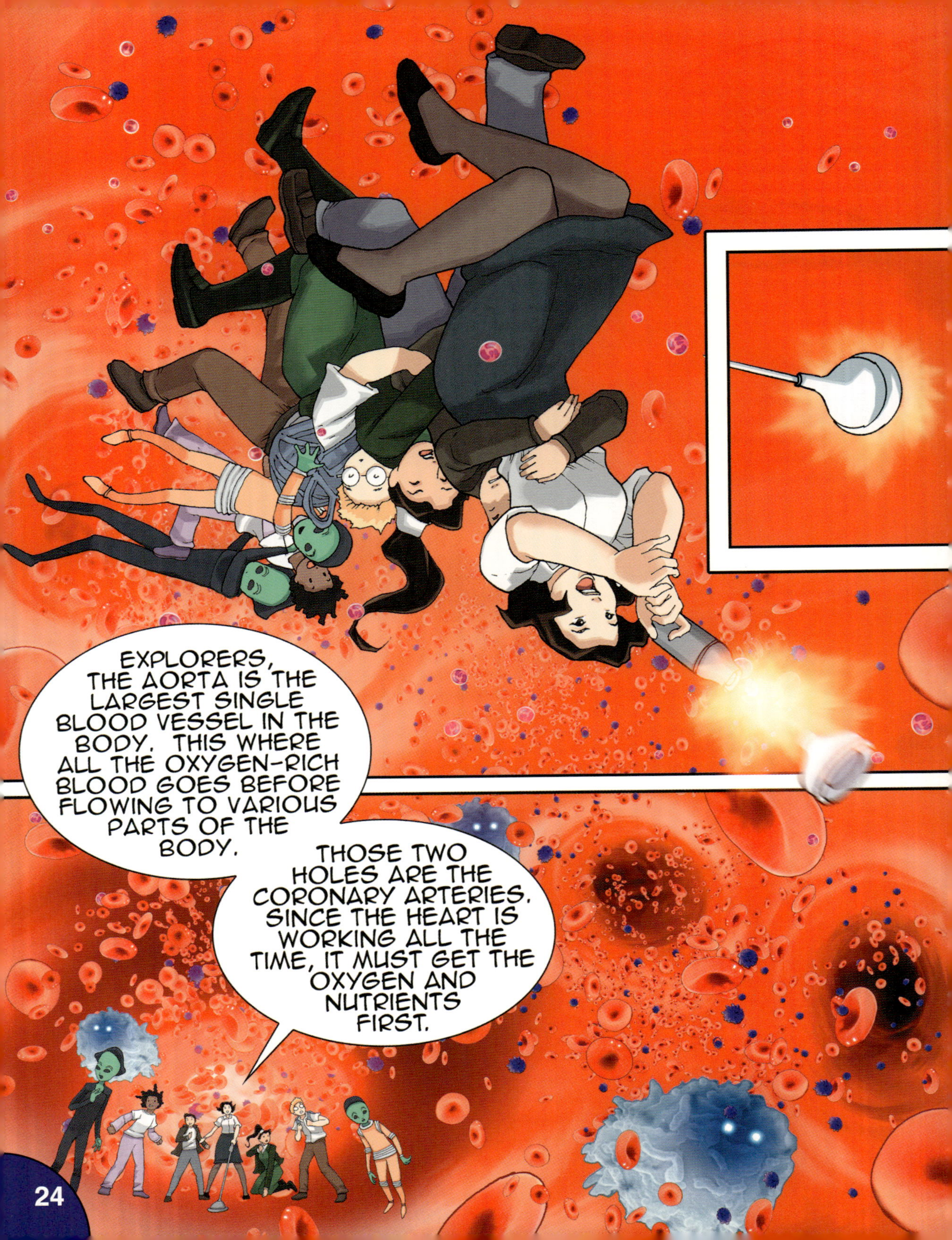
EXPLORERS, THE AORTA IS THE LARGEST SINGLE BLOOD VESSEL IN THE BODY. THIS WHERE ALL THE OXYGEN-RICH BLOOD GOES BEFORE FLOWING TO VARIOUS PARTS OF THE BODY.
THOSE TWO HOLES ARE THE CORONARY ARTERIES. SINCE THE HEART IS WORKING ALL THE TIME, IT MUST GET THE OXYGEN AND NUTRIENTS FIRST.

THERE IS A CORONARY ARTERY THAT GOES TO EACH SIDE OF THE HEART.
THERE ARE BRANCHES OF THE AORTA THAT GO TO THE DIFFERENT PARTS OF THE BODY. THOSE ONES ON TOP ARE GOING TO THE BRAIN, CHEST, AND ARMS.
AND THE AORTA TRAVELS DOWN TO PROVIDE BLOOD TO THE ABDOMEN AND LEGS.
UH-OH, IT'S TIME TO GO! WE DON'T WANT THOSE WHITE BLOOD CELLS TO GET UPSET.
Beep! Beep!

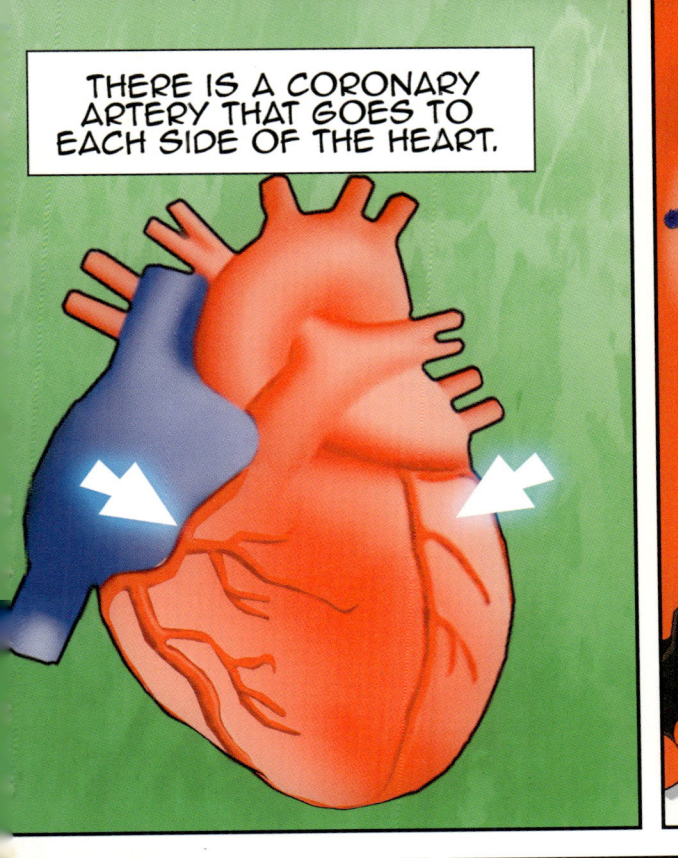

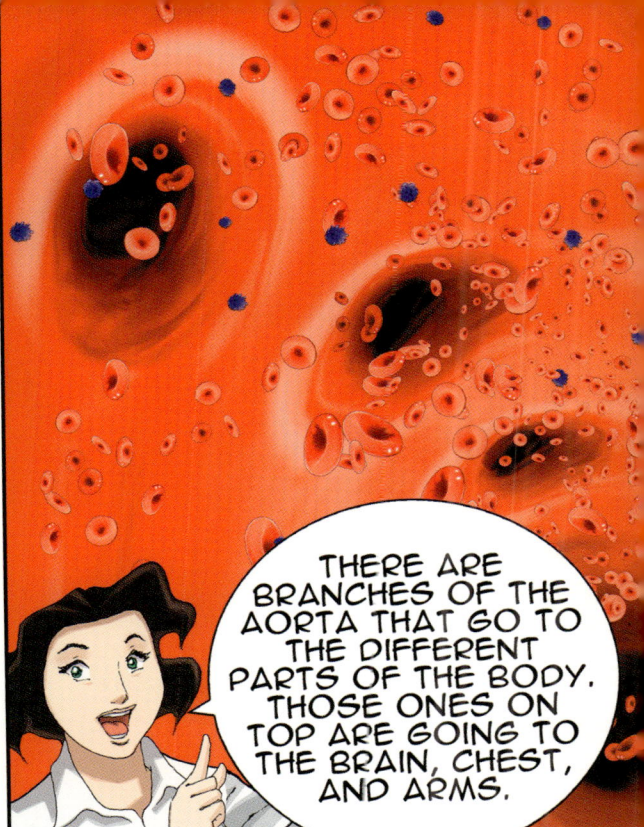

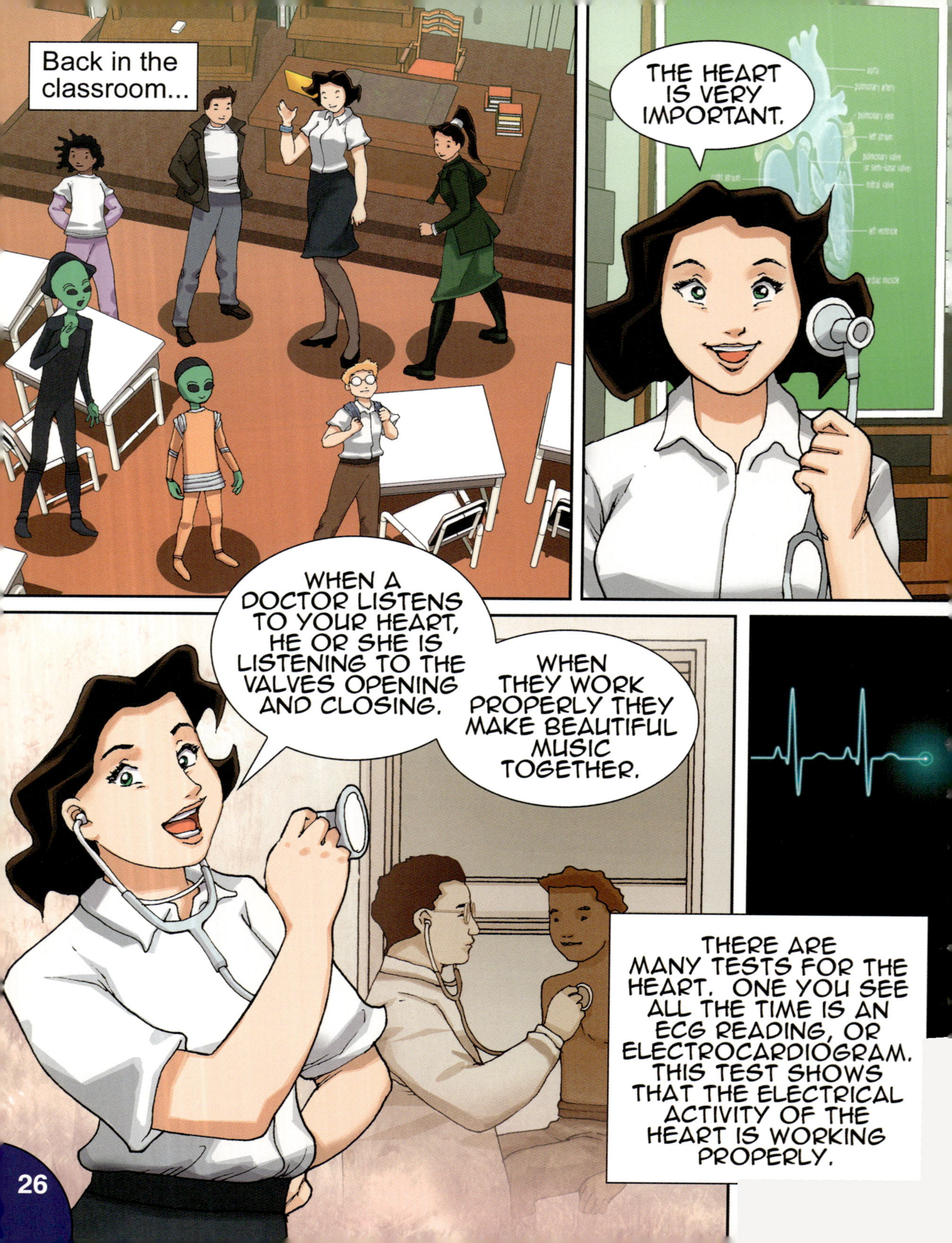
Back in the classroom...
THE HEART IS VERY IMPORTANT.
WHEN A DOCTOR LISTENS TO YOUR HEART, HE OR SHE IS LISTENING TO THE VALVES OPENING AND CLOSING.
WHEN THEY WORK PROPERLY THEY MAKE BEAUTIFUL MUSIC TOGETHER.
THERE ARE MANY TESTS FOR THE HEART. ONE YOU SEE ALL THE TIME IS AN ECG READING, OR ELECTROCARDIOGRAM. THIS TEST SHOWS THAT THE ELECTRICAL ACTIVITY OF THE HEART IS WORKING PROPERLY.

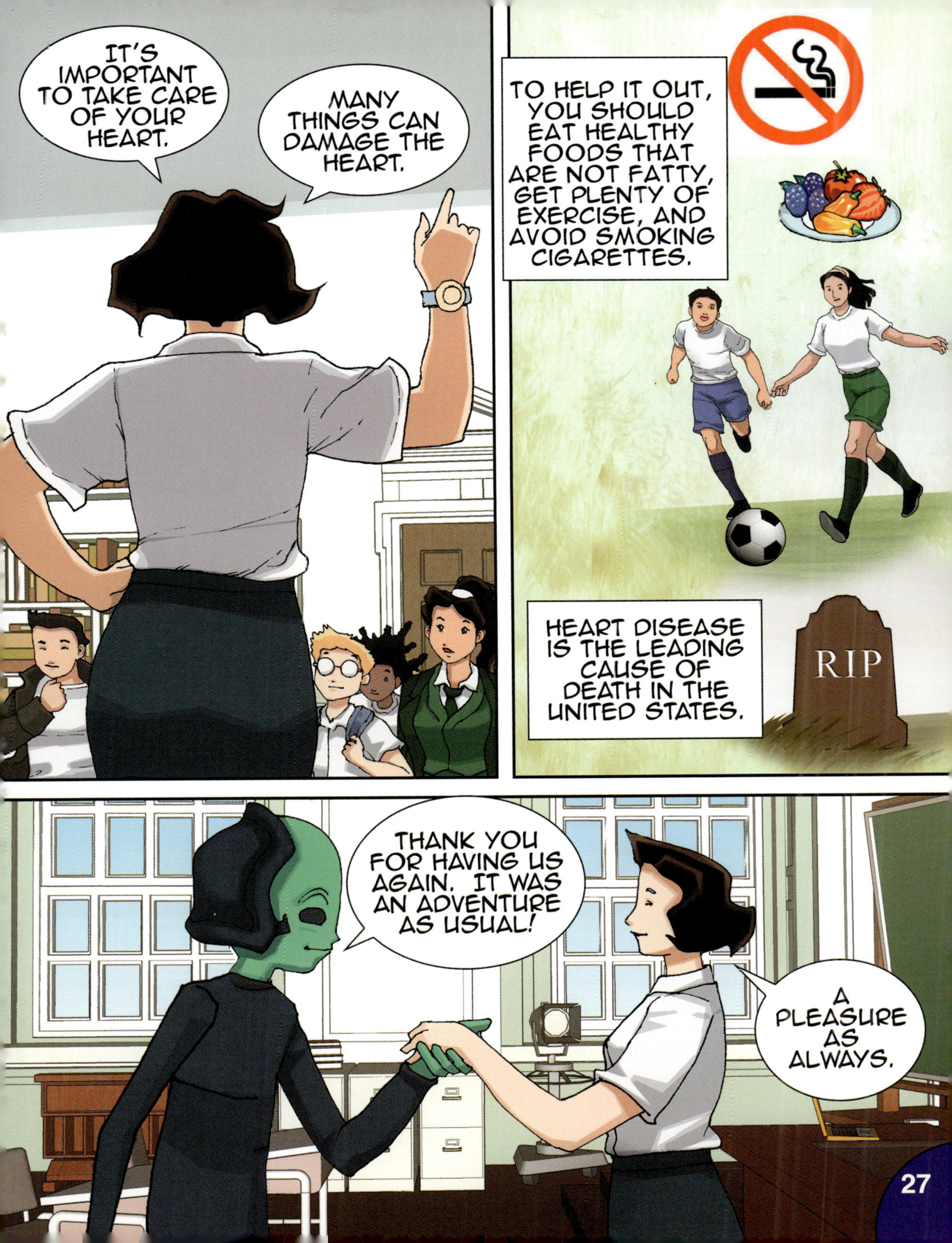
IT'S IMPORTANT TO TAKE CARE OF YOUR HEART.
MANY THINGS CAN DAMAGE THE HEART.
TO HELP IT OUT, YOU SHOULD EAT HEALTHY FOODS THAT ARE NOT FATTY, GET PLENTY OF EXERCISE, AND AVOID SMOKING CIGARETTES.
HEART DISEASE IS THE LEADING CAUSE OF DEATH IN THE UNITED STATES.
RIP
THANK YOU FOR HAVING US AGAIN. IT WAS AN ADVENTURE AS USUAL!
A PLEASURE AS ALWAYS.

The Heart: A Diagram

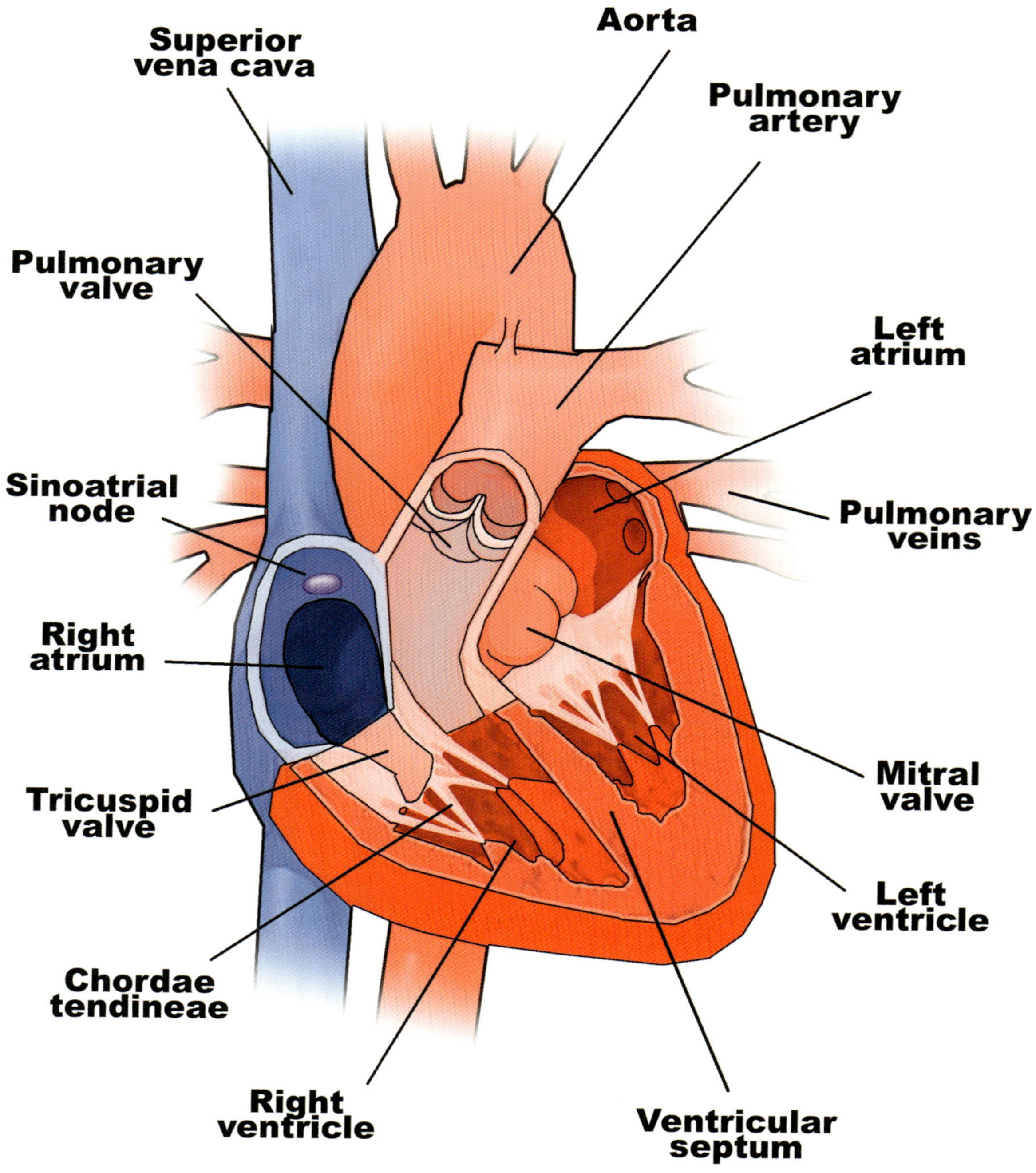
Superior vena cava
Aorta
Pulmonary artery
Pulmonary valve
Left atrium
Sinoatrial node
Pulmonary veins
Right atrium
Mitral valve
Tricuspid valve
Left ventricle
Chordae tendineae
Right ventricle
Ventricular septum

Fun Facts

- There are three main groups of white blood cells—lymphocytes, granulocytes, and monocytes.

- When you say the Pledge of Allegiance and cover your heart, do you cover the left side of your chest? That isn't where your heart is! The heart is actually in the middle of your chest between the lungs.

- It takes about ten seconds for your blood to go from your heart to your big toe when you are exercising!

- Your heart pumps about 100,000 times a day!

- A child has about 60,000 miles (97,000 km) of blood vessels. That's long enough to circle Earth two and a half times!

Glossary

carbon dioxide – a heavy, colorless gas that is created when animals breathe

circulatory system – the system that transports blood within the body. The blood, blood vessels, lymphatics, and heart are all part of the circulatory system.

clot – to go from a fluid to a solid mass because of a complex chemical reaction.

component – a part of something; an ingredient.

immune system – the system that protects the body from foreign substances that can harm it.

organ – a part of an animal or a plant that is composed of several kinds of tissues and that performs a specific function. The heart, liver, gallbladder, and intestines are organs.

plasma – a pale yellow fluid of the blood that is made of water and dissolved nutrients. Plasma carries red and white blood cells through the blood vessels.

puncture – a hole or wound.

syringe – an instrument with a hollow area that is fitted with a plunger and a needle. The plunger pushes fluids from the syringe into the body.

valve – a bodily structure that temporarily closes a passage to permit fluid to move in one direction only.

Web Sites

To learn more about the heart, visit ABDO Group online at www.abdopublishing.com. Web sites about the heart are featured on our Book Links page. These links are routinely monitored and updated to provide the most current information available.

About the Author

Joeming Dunn is both a general practice physician and the owner of one of the largest comic companies in Texas, Antarctic Press. A graduate of Austin College in Sherman and the University of Texas Medical Branch in Galveston, Dunn has currently settled in San Antonio.

Dr. Dunn has written or co-authored texts in both the medical and graphic novel fields. He met his wife, Teresa, in college, and they have two bright and lovely girls, Ashley and Camerin. Ashley has even helped some with his research for these Magic Wagon books.

About the Illustrator

Rod Espinosa is a graphic novel creator, writer, and illustrator. Espinosa was born in the Philippines in Manila. He graduated from the Don Bosco Technical College and the University of Santo Tomas.

Espinosa has worked in advertising, software entertainment, and film. Today, he lives in San Antonio, Texas, and produces stunning graphic novels including *Dinowars, Neotopia, Metadocs, Battle Girlz, Alice in Wonderland, Stop TB!,* and *Prince of Heroes*. His graphic novel *Courageous Princess* was nominated for an Eisner Award.

Index

A
aorta 23, 24, 25

B
blood vessels 7, 9, 18, 19, 24
bone marrow 13

C
capillaries 19
carbon dioxide 11, 12, 20, 21
chordae tendineae 16, 17
circulatory system 7, 8, 9, 10, 12, 13,
 19, 22
clotting 9
coronary artery 24, 25

H
heart disease 27

I
immune system 10

L
left atrium 14, 21
left ventricle 22, 23
lungs 11, 12, 18, 19, 20

M
mitral valve 21, 22, 26

O
oxygen 11, 12, 14, 20, 21, 22, 24, 25

P
papillary muscles 17
plasma 13
platelet 9
pulmonary artery 17, 18
pulmonary valve 17, 18, 26
pulmonary veins 20, 21

R
red blood cell 11
right atrium 14, 15, 21
right ventricle 15, 17, 18, 22

S
septa 22
sinoatrial node 15, 21
superior vena cava 13, 14

T
tricuspid valve 15, 17, 21, 26

W
waste 12
water 13
white blood cell 10, 25